MADISON WHEATLEY

Ambrosia

This edition includes additional content and updates to the original version published under ISBN 978-1644770160.

Second edition

ISBN: 979-8-9923117-1-6

Editing by Rebecca Mikkelson
Proofreading by Brandi Spencer
Cover art by Dee Dee Book Covers

This book was professionally typeset on Reedsy.
Find out more at reedsy.com

Contents

AMBROSIA
DRINK UP. TRANSFORM YOURSELF.
STAY FOREVER.
MADISON WHEATLEY

Content Warning

This title contains the following:

- Discussions of disordered eating, body image struggles, and self-destructive behaviors
- Frequent negative fantasy drug use
- Graphic violence
- Strong language
- Moderate sexual content (implied)
- Miscarriage
- Emotional abuse
- Child abuse
- Attempted suicide

Dedication

To Dale.

You're right—I never should have stopped writing.

Thanks for believing in me when I didn't believe in myself.

Chapter 1

Fat pig. Fat pig. Fat pig.

Jace's ugly words roll around in my head while I stand paralyzed in front of the bathroom mirror. They echo throughout my mind, waking up feelings of self-hatred and disgust. The longer I stare at that hideous figure in the fogged glass, the further my soul seems to sink. But I can't make myself look away.

Can't shut off the voices from the past.

I had come home from work early, only to find someone else's lithe arms coiled around his chest like a white snake. Upon seeing me in the doorway, her arms slithered off his skin as she sprang off the bed.

He rose, half-dressed. Stood next to her in solidarity. The fear in her eyes was absent from his defiant glare.

Normally, I'm able to weaponize my destructive thoughts, normally able to use them as some sick form of "motivation" to drag myself to the gym every morning.

But today is August 3rd. The Anniversary.

Rage bubbled up in my chest, crawled up my throat, and seized control of my brain, shutting down all functions but the message demanding me to fight, to harm, to kill.

"Get. Out."

She sensed the danger in those uttered syllables and slid out from under his arm. Quickly dressing, she flashed sad doe eyes at him before slinking out into the hallway and back into whatever dark hole she'd crawled out of to poison my life.

He stood firm, cross-armed. Unapologetic.

I press my fingers against my temples as if to draw the memory out with my fingertips. "No, not again…" My head swims as I try to suppress the flashback, but it's useless; The Anniversary is in control, an inexorable force that has hijacked my mind and its normal functions, driving me back into the dark.

"Asshole," I seethed, rage and sorrow intermingling like water and blood. "How could you do this to me?"

He raised a dark eyebrow. Looked at me like I was an imbecile.

That look, combined with his damning silence, pushed me over the edge. I stomped over to him and got up in his face, my hands twitching as I resisted the urge to slap him. "How could you? You son of a bitch!"

Fusing my eyelids together tightly, I try once again to push down the memory, but it's no good. The Anniversary has split my soul wide open, and the pain is fresh, raw. All I can do is ride it out, like a sickness.

See, happiness comes easy for some people. Others have to work for it. Then there are people like me, for whom happiness is a pipe dream, more impossible than immortality to obtain. Those of us in that third category have to find a way to live somehow, though. For me, it's the relentless pursuit of distractions.

Throughout the bad years, I've burned through distractions like paper, to varying degrees of success. I went through a phase where I nearly drank myself to death. I've wasted away in front of the TV, shoveling food into my mouth until I don't feel anything at all. But through it all, I've just ended up hating myself more and more.

This year, I'm trying something different, though. Something more positive.

Because, with the sadness that threatens to swallow my soul, distraction isn't enough.

I need an addiction. And for me, nothing does the trick like exercise. When my binging was at its worst, I made an impulse purchase: a basic membership at that hole-in-the-wall gym downtown. As much of a struggle as it was—and still is—for me to make it through a workout session, it didn't take long for the addiction to settle in. Once I get started, the endorphins take over, and I *have* to move.

I move to purge my body of the shame of my binging.

I run to keep the demons out.

Up until now, my system has been working. By throwing myself into a new workout routine, I've found a suitable distraction, one that usually keeps the bad thoughts at bay.

Up until now.

"Can you blame me? I mean, seriously." He scoffed, pushing me away. "It's not my fault you're such a fat pig."

The front door slammed, the sharp sound and his last words resonating in my head. Imprinting.

Hours passed, and I cycled between feeling triumphant and guilty.

Had I gone too far? Had I pushed him away forever? Did I even care?

The phone rang. A police officer.

"There's been an accident. I regret to inform you... "

Regret. There's so much I regret.

I lean over the bathroom sink, gripping it hard to steady myself as the memory runs its course. I shake my head, jaw tight as I steel myself against the shame and the rage and the grief that guts me just as much as it did one year ago today. It's less painful, I find, to stare into the mirror and scrutinize my own appearance.

Ha. Where to begin? My stomach flab spills over my leggings like dough from a busted biscuit tin. My face is dotted with pockmarks from an acne affliction that has lasted well beyond my middle school years. My baby face has yet to flatten out. My wanton curls are ensnared in a taut ponytail, but I know, in a few hours, this look will give way to a halo of tangled frizz.

I started working out a few weeks ago; I've lost three pounds. Three measly, insignificant pounds from a repellent body that takes up far too much space.

While part of me knows I should know better than to be so impatient, I can't help but feel tempted to give up altogether.

The longer I stare at my reflection, the more I hate the image staring back at me. Looking down, tears prick my eyes, and I surrender to that cruel voice I've always tried to snuff out. The voice that says, *It's your fault. You killed him.*

I force myself to face my reflection, my longtime enemy. With a quivering lip, I whisper, "You killed him."

I can't rewrite the past nor untangle its complexities. I can't rewrite myself into someone worth loving. But I can chastise myself, and somehow, that makes me feel better. At least for a while.

The alarm on my phone buzzes, reminding me I should have left the house by now. I turn away from the mirror, taking a few steps toward the bathroom door. I straighten up and sigh. Today is going to suck no matter what, but I know if I stay home, I'll end up binging again.

No. Working out will be my coping skill, my distraction—and my penance.

I fidget with the little cross pendant around my neck. Eyes shut, I imagine strength flowing from the cool silver surface into my skin, coursing throughout my body. But when buried memories bubble to the surface of my mind, I release the pendant and return my glare to the mirror.

"Let's go, fatso," I tell my reflection.

* * *

As soon as I step outside, the Central Arkansas humidity settles all over me like a wet, warm blanket. I instantly feel gross, even more so than I already had. As I'm opening the door to get in, my phone chirps, and my stomach drops when I retrieve it from my pocket to see who's calling.

Dad.

My heart rate quickens, and I just stand there, listening to the phone ring, too baffled and shocked and happy and disgusted to make a decision.

It has been two years since anyone from my family has called me. Two years since that fateful Christmas Eve where my parents hit me with an ultimatum: it was either them or That Boy.

Nope. Not dealing with this today.

My shaky grip tightens around the phone as if to crush it, to silence those shrill electrical alarms that have awakened a tangle of emotions I've tried so hard to ignore.

But there's also this stupid hope in the back of my mind, this childlike voice in the back of my mind incessantly pleading, *Maybe, give him a chance, try, maybe.*

And I just can't. Not today.

With a light squeeze, I shut off the ringer, and the phone ceases in its noise abruptly like a strangled songbird. I feel dizzy after going rounds with my own memories, and when I slide into the driver's seat, I sit there for a long time, trying to no avail to keep myself from thinking. From remembering. From wondering if I've done the right thing or if I've missed my last chance to restore a relationship I'm not even sure holds any value anymore.

1 missed call and 1 voicemail.

As if on cue, my phone vibrates, and the screen lights up to reveal a message. I feel my heart go a little soft as I realize I could listen to my father's voice after two long years of silence from him.

I could do it if I wanted to.

But my mind won't shut the hell up about that one night. I feel weighed down as the pent-up shame and regret and disappointment are dragged up like water from a poisoned well. I sigh, realizing I can't do it. It's been so long, but the pain seems so fresh.

Because he and Julia had ganged up against me about Jace, snapping and condemning me for getting pregnant instead of helping me through it all.

Because I had gone off on them, spewing hate and insults because I was so incredibly scared.

Because Julia had said, *If that's what you think, then you're not welcome in this house anymore.*

Because Dad agreed with her.

So I had clung to That Boy—that heartless, abusive boy—in part out of bitterness over being thrown out of the family. Out of the realization that I had nowhere else to go.

My hands curl around the steering wheel, uneven nails digging into it, making crescent moon shapes into its faux leather skin. Tears sting my eyes, and I can't stop shaking my head because I didn't want to deal with this today, dammit. At last, I put the key in the ignition and switch on the radio. My cheap antenna only picks up static, but it's good enough for a while. Good enough to drown out my own mental cacophony.

Not every day is like this. Most days, I'm able to distract myself well enough, but today, I'm weak. Switching on the car, I search for a functioning radio station; I settle on rap, even though I'm not a fan, then peel out of the parking lot and into the street. A thick layer of fog has settled over Little Rock, so I drive slowly, to the chagrin of the little old lady following me way too closely. She flashes her brights at me and waves a wrinkled hand in anger; I flip her off.

Little by little, I feel the weight of memories slide away, and I can focus on the admittedly mundane present, but as I guide my car toward downtown, a familiar sense of exhaustion overcomes me. It's not easy fighting the past. Distractions help, but I crave more. I want to slip out of my own skin and leave my mind with its toxic memories behind, want to slide into another life, one without baggage and regrets and anxiety.

I want to disappear.

I want to forget.

Chapter 2

As I near the heart of the city, the fog steadily lightens, but I don't pick up the pace, partially because rain has begun to fall, but mostly because Granny Road Rage is still flashing her brights at me. When I guide my car into the left lane to turn into the pharmacy, she blasts her horn; I flash her my best bless-your-heart smile and wave her goodbye before turning into the parking lot, sliding out of my car and racing into the corner pharmacy just as the rain begins to fall in sheets.

Once inside, I waste plenty of time glancing over the display of health food and fitness paraphernalia. In my quest to look for a decent protein bar to eat after my session—because, apparently, that's what you're supposed to do, according to an article I read online—I become so overwhelmed with the options that I think, *Screw it*, snatching up the cheapest one on the shelves before starting toward the checkout line.

A throat clears behind me, stopping me in my tracks.

Turning, I see a young, attractive man who looks like he's in his early thirties or so. He's a bit taller than I am but far skinnier. Not scrawny, though; I can see the outline of his finely sculpted muscles through his black long-sleeved compression shirt. *Damn.* That shirt was made for him. He's holding a protein shake in one hand and pointing at my protein bar with the other.

"Do *not* get PowerUp," he says, grimacing. He's got a distinct Southern accent, authentic and charming. "Has the worst texture. Not to mention, it's fake healthy." He tosses me a smile. "Trust me."

I'm so caught off guard that I can't think of a decent reply. I'm not sure whether I should be grateful for the tip or insulted by his unsolicited advice. In the end, I offer a weak laugh and put the PowerUp back on the shelf. My cheeks flush. "Thanks."

"Let's see." The stranger sidles closer, his gray eyes scanning the shelves, his hand hovering over the selections. His closeness makes my stomach flutter, and though the heat radiating from his body signifies I'm too close, it pains me to think of moving away. I back away slightly, hoping he doesn't notice my flushed cheeks or how loudly my heart slams in my chest. But his cute half-smile assures me that he does.

With his attention diverted, my eyes can't help but roam over him as I check Protein Shake Guy out. His crooked smile hints at mischief, and I wonder if he's a player who sees me as the latest victim in his game. His steel-colored eyes are magnetic, standing out brightly against his sandy, ruffled hair that makes it seem like he just rolled out of bed. There's a confidence in his stance that I envy and yet begrudgingly admire. I wish I were that comfortable in my own skin.

At last, he finds what he's looking for. Stooping down, he retrieves a thick chocolate bar wrapped in orange and gold.

"Now *this one's* amazing," he says, a little grin crawling up his face as he tosses the expensive-looking bar to me. "It's paleo, which means it's great for building muscle after exercise. Not only that, but it tastes great."

"Thanks," I say through another awkward laugh.

He straightens up and smiles at me.

That smile.

"So, I'm assuming you're an expert on this," I say, so he knows I'm capable of more than one-word sentences. I gesture to the intimidating aisle of workout gear and food. "This whole exercise thing."

He shrugs. "I dunno about that; I do all right for myself."

Yeah, you do.

I shuffle on my feet, suddenly feeling self-conscious under his stare.

"You just starting your routine?" he asks.

I nod. "Started about a few weeks ago."

"And you kind of hate it." It's a statement, not a question, as if he's rooting through my thoughts with those intense eyes of his.

"Kind of, yeah," I admit. "Some days more than others."

He nods, leaning casually on the edge of one of the shelves. "Sticking to a routine is rough. It helps if you have a membership at the right gym. Where do you go?"

I look at the floor and hesitate before answering, "Clarke's Gym, down on Route 10."

As I had feared, he looks disgusted. His angular face gets all scrunched up, and he says, "You poor thing."

"I know, I know," I say, holding up my hands. "It's depressing. It smells like mildew and weed. But ten dollars a month? You can't beat that." The moment the words come out, I wish I could take them back. It may not matter in the end what this stranger thinks of me, but for some reason, the idea of his knowing how poor I am makes me feel insecure all over again.

The grossed-out look vanishes from Protein Shake Guy's face. His eyes light up again as if he's had an epiphany. Setting down the drink, he holds up his index finger and moves a half step closer to me. His proximity—close enough that I can smell his piney cologne—makes my breath catch. Flashing me another one of those disarming smiles, he pulls a leather wallet out of his shorts pocket and rifles through it, eventually producing a crisp navy-blue business card with bold yellow lettering.

He holds it out to me, and I take it. Our fingertips brush slightly, and a sudden surge of static electricity shocks me with the contact. It hurts, but I don't react, instead, fixing all my attention on the card.

Mount Olympus Fitness Center, the business card reads. Below that, the slogan: **Be Strong. Be Fierce. Be Immortal**, followed by a phone number and an address I'm not familiar with.

The words send one clear message, that this fitness center would help me craft my doughy body into something better—something *godlike*. The card itself, though—with its thick embossed paper—communicates another: This place is expensive, far too expensive for a waitress at Hungry Harry's BBQ.

"This place," he says, pointing at the card. "It'll change your life."

I stare at the card, and I can't stop my face from revealing my disbelief. Like, does he really just assume I'll be able to afford a place that can afford business cards like this one? He must not be aware of what Wal-Mart brand clothes look like.

The stranger chuckles at my obvious bewilderment. "I know what you're thinking," he says. "Mount Olympus *is* pricey, but they'll work with you. They're new to the area, and you know how that is for small businesses. They're in that stage where they're trying to look good for the community, you know? What I'm trying to say is, if you love it and want to be a member, they'll make it work for you." His eyes shine with excitement. "And you will love it. Trust me."

The stranger steps away, picking up his drink. Taking a few backward steps, he says, "Check it out. Maybe we'll run into each other again." And with that, he makes his way to the checkout line, rings up, and jogs out of the store, leaving me to ponder the bizarre encounter.

Trust me, he'd said. Twice. But that's the thing. I don't trust him. Don't have any reason to. Sure, he's nice, charming, hot as hell.

But that's how Jace was at first too.

It'll change your life, he said.

I'm not going to deny I could use some change in my life.

But is this the right one?

* * *

Back in the car, I place my phone in the cupholder, slipping the fancy business card beneath it. No sooner than I've switched on the ignition does my phone go off again.

Dad, again.

Seriously?

And just like that, those troublesome thoughts flood my mind again, making my head spin and my stomach queasy. The phone seems to ring for ages, and just when I begin to toy with the idea of picking up, it stops. Soon, the screen lights up with a message: **2 missed calls and 1 voicemail.**

I shake my head, and I'm about to pull out of my parking spot when the phone lights up again. A text message. My irritation is replaced with concern as I wonder why he's being so persistent. Has someone gotten hurt? Worse?

Hey, Crystal. Just calling to see how you're doing. I know it's been a while. Worried about you. Love you.

After a moment's hesitation, I reach for the phone. Flipping it over, I see a preview of the text. Heat rises to my cheeks as conflicting thoughts rear up to do battle in my mind once again. My father has always been a liar, at least, ever since he married Julia. He'd told me he would never let anyone replace me, that he would always be there for me. Yet time after time throughout my childhood, he would side with her whenever, even as she bullied me for my weight, for my interests, for merely existing. He was supposed to defend me, but he never took my side. Not even when I needed him most.

"I know it's been a while." Yeah, no shit, it has. And too much has happened.

No. He's not really worried about me. He's only clearing his conscience. This way, he can say he tried and place the blame on me for not answering. That's just how he is. At least, that's what Julia has turned him into.

I know better than to fall for this. The words "I love you" are just some cheap mask he hides behind. And why now? After years of silence, how am I supposed to believe that he's had a change of heart?

Forget him.

I put away the phone, flicking it to silent mode. My fingertips brush the business card, and I pick it up again.

My eyes rest on the text. ***Be Strong. Be Fierce. Be Immortal.***

"Maybe," I say as Protein Shake Guy's testimonial replays in my head, reminding me that, at this point in life, I need more than a mere distraction.

I need a real change.

Taking a deep breath, I pick up the business card and plug the address into my phone's GPS, hoping for the best.

Chapter 3

The rain has let up, and I'm just nearing the outer edge of the city when my phone lights up again. I'm stopped at an intersection, and I'm half tempted to ignore it, thinking it's Dad again. I check anyway, though, and roll my eyes and groan when I see a wall of texts from Felicia, my boss.

9-1-1!!!

KAREN QUIT!!!

CAN U COME IN??? PLS???

I shake my head. Felicia always begins such texts with "9-1-1," hoping it will incite her employees to the same state of frenzy she's known for. I'm at the point where those numbers have lost the urgency they used to signify for me.

Good for Karen, I think, fantasizing about the day when *I'll* finally be able to bid farewell to Hungry Harry's BBQ for good. I knew she'd been flirting with the idea of quitting, but I didn't know she'd found a replacement job already.

The light changes, and I turn off the GPS, pulling into the U-turn lane and heading toward home so I can change from my workout clothes into that dreadful pink-and-white Hungry Harry's uniform.

I guess changing my life will have to wait.

* * *

Despite my internally mocking Felicia's panic-filled text, the only thing I can think when I step into Hungry Harry's is, *9-1-1!* The place is packed, uncharacteristically so for a gloomy Saturday afternoon like today. Teenage boys gather around booths, guffawing and stuffing their faces while the adults supervising them try to keep them in line. A few elderly guests, clearly not part of the group the teens belong to, shoot judgmental glares at the youths.

Felicia ambles toward me, strands of her dark hair sticking up everywhere and her worried eyes two wide honey-colored disks.

"State basketball tournament," she explains, chipped nails fiddling with the stack of menus she holds. "Of all days, Karen. She did this on purpose to get back at me, I swear to God."

That doesn't sound like Karen, but I know better than to argue with Felicia when she's feeling this way. "How can I help?"

She points to two separate booths, both populated by a cluster of rowdy teenagers; a middle-aged man, maybe a coach, is goofing off with both tables at once. Felicia hands me the stack of menus emblazoned with Hungry Harry's signature image: a smiling family of cartoon pigs sitting down to enjoy Hungry Harry's famous pulled pork sandwiches. Yes, it's messed up, and no, they're not going to change it anytime soon. These cute little pork-loving cannibals are plastered all over the walls of Hungry Harry's. One of the more ridiculous examples, a strangely sexualized female pig with big Dolly Parton hair and a short, skin-tight rendition of the Hungry Harry's waitress uniform, hangs between the two tables I'm about to serve, winking. Just ew.

"You're a lifesaver," she says, on the verge of tears as she rushes to the back of the restaurant, tripping over her own feet in her hurry.

I look toward the group of boys, who are trying unsuccessfully to suppress their laughter at Felicia's act of clumsiness. Their coach, a balding, ginger-haired man, tells them all to knock it off, lightly smacking one kid in the back of the head for emphasis. This only makes the kids laugh harder and more boisterously.

Why did it have to be teenagers? I grit my teeth and approach the booths, plastering on my best tip-winning smile. I greet them and take their orders.

One boy changes his mind several times before settling on the bacon cheeseburger platter. Another lets out a huge fart, which causes the other boys to fall into fits of hysterical laughter. The coach continually tells them to be quiet through his own distracting laughter.

My grip tightens around the pen in my left hand. *Tip. Winning. Smile.*

After what seems like hours, I take their orders and disappear into the back room, where Cici is manning the grill. I pin up the order sheet, taking a deep breath to allow myself a moment of reprieve.

"Karen picked a hell of a day to leave." With a flick of her skinny wrist, she flips a burger, and then places a slice of cheese on it before moving on to the next one. "These teenagers, man. Freakin' goblins."

"Weren't you a teenager, like, two months ago?" For the first time today, I feel somewhat relaxed. Cici and her humor are always a breath of fresh air.

She ignores my observation, casting a disdainful stare through the kitchen window. "So rude. Sometimes I just wanna—"

"Spit in their food, I know." Cici has this strange fixation on the whole stereotype about servers and cooks spitting in rude customers' food. She's never done this herself, but she sure likes to talk about doing it—at least, when Felicia's not in earshot. Such talk would surely result in a tirade from our boss.

"Just once!" The smell of burning meat makes Cici snap out of her disgusting revenge fantasy, and she begins flipping burgers again.

"Well, maybe this will be your lucky day," I say as I leave the kitchen.

* * *

Not all of the teenagers are bad, to be fair. Certainly not bad enough for me to consider desecrating their precious pulled pork sandwiches. This shift is still a hot mess, though, and before long, my happiness for Karen has turned to a toxic mixture of resentment and envy. I wait on what feels like hundreds of customers, zipping in and out of the kitchen, just trying to keep up with everything. At one point, I deliver the wrong order to the wrong table; they don't yell at me, thankfully, but the irritation is evident, so much so that I can tell they're not going to tip me.

And then there are *those* tables. The ones with the basketball players and their man-child of a coach. In my haste to make everyone in the restaurant happy at once, especially Felicia, I neglect to refill their drinks promptly. And when the coach yells, "Hey!" and waves me over, I'm already on edge.

"How may I help you?" My tip-winning smile has disappeared, lost somewhere between the kitchen and the table with the perpetually crying twin toddlers, but I try my best to be friendly as I wait for this man's criticism.

He doesn't even give me the courtesy of telling me what I did wrong. Not with words, anyway. He simply points to his empty cups, staring at me with his hard, cruel eyes. The basketball boys flash each other meaningful looks, and my stomach churns as I realize that while I've been running around like a crazy person trying to keep this place afloat, these people have been shit-talking me.

I bite back the stream of angry words that threatens to spill over and begin collecting the plastic cups. "I'm very sorry, sir," I say. Then I plaster on my fake smile and decide to try diffusing the situation with humor. I'm too flustered to manage anything other than, "Hectic day, isn't it? Everyone and their mother decided to come here today."

The coach smiles, but there's no warmth in it. A few of the basketball boys snicker. One rolls his eyes.

When I'm safely behind the walls of the kitchen, I close my eyes and squeeze my necklace for a few seconds until my head stops pounding. When the memories threaten to crawl back, I open my eyes and attempt to reintegrate myself into my surroundings; Felicia is berating Cici for not cooking fast enough. Cici is ignoring her, offering only "mhm"s and the occasional "yes, ma'am" as she mans the grill. The tension in the air is palpable as servers dash in and out of the doors, some muttering profanities under their breath, some making snide remarks about customers, one crying and trying to hide it.

Thanks a lot, Karen.

As I make my way to the soda machine and refill my table's drinks, I can feel myself unraveling, as if my mind's logical functions are steadily shutting down, replaced by the overwhelm of emotion. It's an all too familiar feeling, one that had made me lash out when I was with Jace. Made me binge eat shortly after his death. Made me make impulsive, idiotic decisions time and time again. I take a deep breath, trying to focus on the sound of the soda emptying into the cups. Trying to ground myself in the present.

But then I glance out of the kitchen window, catching a glimpse of my table. They're back at it again with their rowdy joking, and now and again, look impatiently toward the kitchen door.

I'm on the last glass when I notice it. One kid pointing at the wall—pointing at the "sexy" pig. I don't think anything of it until the other boys—*and* the coach—erupt in laughter, and one of them says, "SHE TOTALLY DOES!" Everyone else at the table hushes him, a few casting nervous glances to the door.

My head swims. My face burns, and I don't know whether to cry or take Cici's advice and spit in their food.

Because I know I'm not overreacting. I can tell when I'm being insulted behind my back.

I can tell when someone's mocking me for my appearance. My weight.

For years, it was all I knew.

When sweet tea overflows from the glass and covers my fingers, I snap out of it. Dumping some of the tea out, I arrange the glasses on a tray, trudging toward the serving room.

"Psst!"

I turn to see Cici, who must know I'm upset without knowing why.

She holds up an empty plate and hocks an imaginary loogie into it.

I manage a shaky smile, then step out of the kitchen.

As I cross the restaurant floor, I still feel unhinged, and with every step toward the kids and the man-child, that fog of emotion clouding my mind only intensifies. Breathing deeply, I tell myself to just ignore them, to let it all roll off my back, that it doesn't matter what some random strangers think of me. *Tip-winning smile, tip-winning smile...* Even though I know there's no chance in hell I'm getting a tip from these people.

But as I arrive at their table, they're all looking at me. Not in that expectant way some customers look at the person who is supposed to bring them their food. No, they're *evaluating* me. The weight in their gazes is palpable.

One kid glances from me to the sexy pig and back to me. He nods to the kid next to him.

Another murmurs, "Yeah, I see it."

One says, "Y'all are childish," occupying himself with his cell phone.

But it's the coach who sets me off. He says nothing. Just exchanges glances with the one who's pointed out the sexy pig in the first place, then faces me. He laughs—a single, scornful note—and smirks at me like he's looking at the most pathetic creature on earth.

I am a pot about to boil over, but I grit my teeth and pass out their drinks. It takes every ounce of strength within me not to slam the cups on the table.

"*Ex-cuse* me," the coach says when he samples his drink. "This is supposed to be *un*sweet tea, not sweet tea."

All eyes at the table look away as the coach scolds me like I'm a very young, very stupid child.

"I'm sorry, sir," I say, picking up the cup, so flustered that I nearly knock over one kid's Dr. Pepper in the process.

My mind is shutting down.

"What is wrong with you?" The coach's voice is soft but dripping with disdain. "You really don't know what you're doing, do you?"

I know I should leave. I should tell Felicia to take over. Just apologize and get the hell out of here.

But there's something about the coach's voice that makes my feet stick to the floor. Something about the snark, the disgust. The pure, unadulterated haughtiness with which this man speaks to me. I feel chills, as though Jace himself is speaking to me from beyond the grave, using this random guy as his vessel. Even now, still criticizing.

Even now, still reminding me that I'm worthless.

The coach snaps his fingers in my face, and I jump. "Hello!" he snaps. "Wake the hell up, and fix my order!"

The last cords holding me together snap. I smile, but not for tips this time.

"So sorry," I croon with false sweetness, not bothering to tack on "sir" at the end. "Let's get rid of this sweet tea."

And I don't spit in his drink, even though, in my periphery, I can see Cici watching me through the kitchen window.

But I do dump the abhorrent sweet tea all over his polo and khakis.

* * *

Frantic Felicia has lost all her nervous energy. After dealing with a full house of customers, not to mention the fallout from the stunt I had pulled, she's completely spent.

Needless to say, the coach lost it when I dumped tea all over him. He jumped out of his seat quick enough to make his table shudder and tried to grab me, breathing out curses and threats all the while. Another server stepped between him and me, though, and somehow, magically, calmed him enough to enable me to escape back into the kitchen. Felicia came over and handled the furious customer, taking over for me like I should have had her do in the first place. He didn't give her a tip.

Now I'm sitting in Felicia's tiny immaculate office at the end of the day, helpless as she rubs her temples and draws deep breaths in an attempt to soothe herself. I know for a fact that it's over, that I'm doomed. Felicia is a firm believer that "the customer is always right." She's the type to bend over backward for The Customer and his ridiculous requests and abuse, and she certainly expects her employees to do the same.

Just get it over with, I think, my fingers laced tightly together and my foot tapping at a nervous pace. *I know what you're going to say, just say it!*

"Why, Crystal?" Her voice is almost pleading, lacking its usual strain. "What on earth were you thinking?"

I can't meet her gaze because I know she wouldn't believe the truth. Wouldn't accept it as a valid excuse.

"What could that man have said that was so horrible?" Felicia seems genuinely shocked that customers are capable of saying and doing things that warrant a good tea-spilling. Or worse.

"It's not so much what he said. It's how he said it." If this is to be my last conversation with Felicia, then she at least deserves to hear the truth. "It made me think of someone..."

Her expression softens. "Someone who hurt you," she says.

"Yeah." *Someone who hurt me. Someone I hurt. Someone I killed.*

Felicia looks out the window as if to find the answer to her dilemma there. She looks thoughtful as she watches the raindrops chase each other on the glass.

"I'm sorry." The apology feels weak. I'm not really sorry for what I did, but I am sorry for how it's affecting Felicia and her business.

"I know," she says. "And I'm not gonna fire you. I do think you need to...lay low for a while."

* * *

Turns out that "lay low for a while" is a polite way of saying "suspended without pay." For a week, to be exact.

Driving home after receiving my sentence, I ponder what this suspension means for me.

It means an interrupted routine.

It means time alone. Time to think. Time to get swallowed up in memories and regrets.

And I'm afraid.

I almost wish she had fired me. If she had, I'd have to look for a new job, and the stress of that task would keep my mind off things.

The rain falls in sheets, and thunder makes the pavement shake as I pull into the parking lot of my apartment around 9:45 that night. As I gather my things, my fingers find the business card I'd forgotten about in the stress of the day. Mount Olympus Fitness Center.

I crack the driver's door open, and the car floods with light. I look over the business card. Protein Shake Guy said that Mount Olympus would "work with me" on the pricing, that they're trying hard to make themselves "look good to the community." Maybe I won't be able to afford this place long-term, but maybe they'll offer me a free trial that will keep me occupied throughout my suspension.

Pocketing the card and my phone, I exit my car and rush through the storm into my apartment. Too tired to think, I collapse in bed and dream all night of Jace and the sexy pig and the coach and Dad and "*fat pig, fat pig..."*

But I wake up early that next morning, energized. Hopeful. Because I have a plan.

Chapter 4

The following morning, I'm behind the wheel of my car, following the phone GPS's directions to the Mount Olympus Fitness Center. It feels weird not going to my usual haunt, that tiny storefront gym that reeks of disappointment. And while my head is reeling with doubts about this new place, Protein Shake Guy's testimonial keeps me driving, particularly the part where he suggested they would "work with me" when it comes to the cost. I roll my eyes at the idea of being some organization's pity project, but I drive on. I know I need one hell of a distraction if I'm going to survive this week.

The diminutive Little Rock skyline gradually flattens, and before long, I'm surrounded by soybean fields. While Arkansas certainly has its fair share of rural landscapes, I'm not used to venturing so far from the city. My fingernails drum against the steering wheel. *What if this is all a prank...or worse?*

After a good forty-five minutes, a massive yellow and navy blue building rises over the horizon like a concrete sun. Its parking lot is packed, and I'm forced to park in the very back of the lot. I frown at the rows of cars suggesting that this place should be abuzz with activity; I hate working out with a lot of eyes watching me. Despite the cars, an eerie silence hangs over the lot. I don't see anyone entering or leaving their vehicles, and I get the feeling that I've arrived unfashionably late to a party. Breathing deeply to cleanse myself of nervousness, I take a couple steps toward the building.

And that's when my phone rings.

Dad, I think without looking at the screen. When the caller ID confirms my suspicion, my fingers hover over the touchscreen. I've resolved not to talk to him, but the temptation is there all the same.

I could tell him off, I think. *I could release all that frustration and pain I've let build up after all these years.*

Maybe that'll make me feel better.

I press the answer button. "Yeah." My greeting is clipped.

There's a pause on the other end, as if he's confused by my response. "Crystal?"

"Yeah. It's me."

His voice sounds strangely soft and tearful, creating an eerie contrast between my cold tone and his emotional one. "Why haven't you been answering?"

And that just about does it for me. "Why haven't I been answering? Where have you been over the past two years?"

Another pause. "I called yesterday because I knew it was a hard day for you..."

A one-note laugh that doesn't sound like me escapes my throat. "Yeah well, maybe yesterday wouldn't have happened if not for you. If you hadn't pushed me out of your life. If you hadn't listened to that bitch wife of yours."

"Don't you dare talk about her that way!" There's a hint of sadness mixed in with his rage, making me almost regret my insult. Almost.

It takes me a moment to gather the strength to say the next words without crying. "I needed you, Dad. Even if you didn't agree with my choices...I'm still your daughter."

I think about all the nights when I'd cradled the phone in my hand while Jace snored next to me, sleeping peacefully while I stayed up late nursing the emotional wounds he'd left me. Night after night, I thought,

Dad would know what to do. Dad needs to know what's happening.

And night after night, I set down the phone on my nightstand and cried because it was too late to run back to him now. He had made it abundantly clear: I'm not part of the family anymore.

Dad's voice is quiet but rough like sandpaper. "I thought I was doing the right thing," he says. "Tough love."

Blinking back tears, I lean up against my car, facing away from the gym. "So did I." *Stupid love.*

I hang up after a long silence. It's clear he wants to make things right between the two of us, but that's not something that can be done over the phone. If he really did care, he'd leave his Nashville penthouse for a few hours and have this conversation with me face to face. But that's not really Dad's thing. He prefers to look like he cares.

I drift across the parking lot in a daze, reeling from that brief conversation.

That was it. My fists ball up as I fight back tears. That was what I waited two years for.

I quicken my pace as if the speed will shake off all my uneasy feelings. I'm not going to make it through this week unless I block out emotions like this. So when I wrench open the doors to the fitness center and start toward the reception desk, I make sure to block Dad's number on my phone.

Sorry, Dad, I think. *Maybe someday, but not today.*

"Well, hey there!" A bright female voice snaps me out of my musing. Looking up, I see a petite receptionist with Reba McEntire hair, waving at me from behind the large desk that encircles her like a city wall. She's positively beaming as she watches my approach, and I can't help but find it a bit unsettling. No one should be *this* happy at work, especially not at 7 a.m. on a Sunday.

"Come on in!" she says, beckoning toward me, despite the fact that I'm already "coming on in." I humor her and walk a little faster, in hopes that this will make her calm the hell down. As soon as I'm close enough, her hand shoots across the desk. "I'm Sasha. Welcome to Mount Olympus!"

I shake her hand and introduce myself. "Crystal." *That grip!* She releases her vice-like grip and settles back into her chair, which swivels slightly at the impact. "So what brings you here today?"

For half a second, I consider being smart with her because that's kind of a dumb question. Instead, I tell her about my encounter with Protein Shake Guy and how he recommended this place. "I didn't get his name," I say at the end of my story. "He's definitely a member, though. Very…enthusiastic?" I have to stop myself from saying "nerdy." I mean, who carries around workout center business cards in their wallet?

Sasha smiles and clicks her mouse a few times before opening a desk drawer and rummaging through it, her red hair bouncing with every movement. "We've found that word-of-mouth is the best form of advertisement," she says. "Our members love it here, and I know you will too."

Her confidence in how much I'll love this place makes me think of Protein Shake Guy. All this hype should be reassuring, but something about it makes me uneasy.

She gives me a trifold brochure, which contains a map of the huge facility and a list of its amenities. Swimming pools. Weight rooms. Walking tracks. Saunas and steam rooms. Masseuses and hot tubs. Open 24/7. All free, at least for this week, Sasha explains.

Whoa. Maybe I will love it here. I gape at the brochure, and excitement bubbles inside me as I try to figure out where I even want to start. My eyes fall to the price of membership at the bottom, and I have to fight to keep my jaw from dropping. *Three hundred a month? That's almost as high as my rent!*

I set the brochure on the counter, slowly pushing it toward Sasha. "Sorry for wasting your time. This place is incredible, but there's no way I can afford to be a member here."

Sasha shakes her head, unfazed by my reaction. "Back page," she says, pointing to the brochure.

I flip over the glossy paper, and in the center of the brochure is a chart labeled "Discounts." Before I have a chance to read it myself, Sasha hovers over me and points at the chart.

"New member discount, 25% for the first year," she explains. She reaches across the desk and grabs a pen, then begins scribbling numbers on a clear space on the brochure. "So that shaves off $75."

So I'm down to $225 now. That's nowhere near good enough.

"You were referred by a member, which takes off another $50." She does the subtraction on the paper before asking, "Are you in the military?" she asks. "Or do you have a military spouse?"

"Neither," I say, my heart sinking as I realize she must have reached the last available discount. "$175 is a lot better than $300," I tell her. "But, see, I'm a waitress." *A waitress who's currently losing an entire week's worth of pay.* "I just don't think I can manage another heavy bill like that."

Sasha's silver eyes stare at me, emotionless as if waiting to hear more from me. Before long, her silence is so uncomfortable that words start spilling out without my permission.

"I want this, Sasha," I say. "I really do. I want—I *need* to lose weight. I hate the way I look, the way I feel..." I stop myself before I get too deep in my feelings.

"I understand," Sasha says, reaching out her petite hand to gently cover mine. "And...after fighting bravely for your country, I think you deserve to do something for yourself, don't you?"

It takes a minute to process what she's saying, and once I do, I slide my hand out from under hers. "No, no...don't do that," I say, disgust and hope intermingling at Sasha's implied solution to my problem.

But she's already subtracting from the discounted price. "There." She points to the new price with a perfectly manicured fingernail. "Better?"

From $300 a month down to $90 a month, as if by magic.

Sasha waits for my answer, but the words won't come out.

Chapter 5

I amble out of the lobby in a fog, trying to sort out my conflicting emotions. On the one hand, Sasha's doing me a huge favor, probably risking getting herself in trouble to get me that military discount. On the other hand, I feel guilty for accepting it, even if she didn't give me much choice in the matter; if I sign up with her, I'm getting that discount whether I like it or not.

Then there's the matter of my monthly payment. Even if it's heavily discounted, $90 a month is still a huge blow to my already tight budget. It's doable but only barely so.

Rounding a corner toward the women's locker room, I nearly collide with a yellow-clad Mount Olympus staff member carrying a tray of small cups like the kind they use to offer free samples in a mall food court. I flatten myself against the wall and watch in horror as the middle-aged lady sways, nearly dropping the tray and the sample cups along with it. When at last she regains her balance, I let go of the breath I've been holding.

"I'm so sorry," I say, putting a hand over my chest. "Wasn't paying attention."

The lady grins and waves a hand. "Don't worry about it, sweetie." I start to walk off, but she stops me with, "You new here? I'm Clarissa."

"Crystal," I say, determined to keep this conversation short. "Nice to meet you."

She holds the tray of plastic cups filled with a clear liquid closer to me. "Would you like to sample our sports drink, Ambrosia? We're beta-testing it and would greatly appreciate your feedback."

I'm not opposed to free samples, but I've never been a huge fan of sports drinks. "No, thanks," I say, continuing toward the locker room. "Maybe another time, though."

Clarissa smiles. "See you around."

Mount Olympus... Ambrosia... I ponder the somewhat pretentious names as I make my way down the tiled corridor. I just hope this place is half as divine as these people think it is.

* * *

It's a good workout, don't get me wrong. Mount Olympus certainly has the "vibe" that I'm looking for in a fitness center. It's refreshing to be away from that gray-walled, stinky-sock-smelling hole in the wall known as Clarke's Gym. But as I pump my limbs to the rhythm of the elliptical machine, I can't help but think that, other than the fact that instead of a timer, it has a cute animated hourglass, it's not much different from the elliptical I use at Clarke's. Weird. And certainly not worth $90 a month.

A gym's a gym, I think, slipping earbuds into my ears and trying to open my music streaming app. I scowl, opening and closing the app as my phone struggles to connect. *At least Clarke's has functioning Wi-Fi.*

Giving up, I pocket my earbuds and settle for the weird music flooding from the speakers on the wall. It's some kind of electronic beat, punctuated with unintelligible lyrics. As my workout intensifies and weakness begins to settle in, I focus on trying to identify the songs or even their genres. Once or twice, I catch a snippet that sounds vaguely like a song I'm familiar with, but I can never be sure. One thing's for certain: I love the way it sounds. I love the way it ebbs and flows and propels me into stride after stride, giving me the second wind I need to get through the workout.

When the last of the digital sand empties into the bottom of the hourglass on the screen, I wipe my brow and smile at my accomplishments: 300-something calories burned, as usual. My heart sinks when I realize that this is a drop in the bucket compared to the progress I have to make. Once again, I tell myself that it's worthless and that I should give up altogether.

And that's when I see him: Protein Shake Guy, a white towel slung over his neck as he chats it up with a custodian. Instead of a compression shirt, today he's wearing this dark T-shirt with the sleeves cut out so low that the sides of his sculpted abs are visible. My heartbeat races as I'm torn between the desire to run up to him or to sneak away before I catch his attention.

Of course, he starts walking toward me before I have the chance to make up my mind. His eyes light up when they meet mine, freezing me in place as he approaches me.

"Thought I'd find you here." There it is again, that crooked smile that turns my legs to jelly. "Didn't think it'd be so soon."

"I've got a week off from work." My voice sounds weirdly high and tentative. "Figured now was as good a time as any to check this place out."

"And? Verdict?" He grins from ear to ear, leaning in expectantly.

"It's all right," I say. "Might be a little too rich for my blood." My eyes drop to my scuffed sneakers at the admission.

He cocks his head toward the hallway connecting the weight room with the rest of the facility. "You tried the pool yet?"

"Not yet." Up until now, I've been considering ducking out before trying any of the other amenities. Why give myself a taste of luxury I know I can't afford?

"Let's go."

I know better than to follow. But it's almost painful watching him go. "Sure, I'll join you," I blurt out. When he turns, I add, "But first, you have to tell me your name."

* * *

It's just Rory. That's it. Not that that's a bad name, just not at all what I was expecting. I'm kind of relieved that it's not Apollo or Zeus or something ridiculous like that.

Mount Olympus boasts two saltwater pools: a fifty-meter lap pool and a smaller therapy pool. Rory and I sink into the warmth of the therapy pool. We're its only occupants other than a small group of elderly women doing water aerobics exercises on the other end. The warm salt water is just what my tense muscles need; I stretch my arms out on the pool deck and let the rest of my body float on top of the water, closing my eyes.

"This is the life," I say through a dreamy sigh. "I don't want to leave."

Rory chuckles. "That's the beauty of a 24-hour gym," he says. "You can stay as long as you'd like."

As long as you like. I smile, comforted by the words.

A long, tranquil moment passes. Finally, I plant my feet on the bottom of the pool and turn to face Rory. "So what's your story?" I ask, leaning up against the pool wall. "How'd you stumble upon this place?"

"Friend recommended it." Rory looks away, gazing across the still waters toward the crowded lap pool. "I dunno... I've got some stuff going on in my life. Sometimes...I just have to blow off steam, you know? Working out helps."

It's good to know I'm not the only one who feels that way. "I get it," I say. "This particular time of year is always rough for me."

For a moment, we're silent, each of us lost in the memories we try to hide from. After a while, though, I begin to wonder how long I've been in Mount Olympus. Dabbing my hand on a nearby towel, I pick up my phone and have to hold back my gasp.

"It's eleven fifteen already?" How have I been here for four hours?

"Time flies," replies with a shrug as I climb the staircase leading out of the pool. "What's the rush?"

Then I remember that I have nothing going on. Nothing to look forward to. Still, I can't just stay here forever. "Just got some stuff to do at home," I lie.

Rory nods in such a way that he looks like he's fighting sleep. "Maybe I'll see you around?" He gives me that mischievous half-smile, making my heart flutter again.

"I hope so," I tell him before heading toward the locker room. The farther I drift from him, the harder it seems to make my heavy feet move.

* * *

As soon as I step out of that warm paradise, I begin to regret my decision. A steady downpour of cold rain slaps at my skin, and I curse myself for not bringing an umbrella as I rush across the parking lot.

But despite the weather, I feel great—alive. That weird Mount Olympus music still pumps through my head, making the walk through the torrential downpour slightly more bearable. And when I finally slide into my car, my brief conversation with Rory replays in my head, making my stomach do somersaults as I recall what that smile of his does to me.

Maybe I'm too poor to afford this place, I think, backing my car out of the parking spot. *But I'd be stupid not to enjoy it for free while I can.*

* * *

So I'm back again the next day, bright and early at six a.m. after a night of fitful sleep; I hadn't been able to quiet my mind down, and when I finally did sleep, a cocktail of anxiety and grief and infatuation resulted in a fitful night of vivid dreas.

I'm surprised to see Sasha still working reception when I return, and she's overjoyed to see me. "You're back!"

"Couldn't sleep," I say, adjusting the gym bag strap slung over my shoulder. With that, I drift past her without letting her bait me into more small talk. *Geez, lady, what did you put in your coffee this morning?*

Brushing past Clarissa and her free samples—I guess that's what she does here. What I wouldn't give to have a job as easy as passing out little plastic cups all day—I make my way back into the room with the exercise machines. After doing a session on the elliptical, I find I still have energy to burn, so I climb the stairs and do some laps on the walking track.

The music is louder up here. The electronic pulsing and the high tempo moves me forward, and I try to match my steps to the beat of the song—whatever it is. I usually find walking boring, but I'm finding it difficult to stop, even as my legs cramp up, and I look at my phone to realize that a full hour has passed.

When I can't ignore the pain in my legs anymore, I finally force myself to step off the track. My feet drag, hesitant. I don't want to leave... An image of my dark, lonely apartment flashes in my mind.

"Find something else to do," I say, walking away from the track.

After a few moments of aimless walking, I come across a huge room split into three sections: One is lined with various climbing walls. The floor of the second section is made of trampolines, on which gym members are flying and somersaulting through the air. The third contains an obstacle course of sorts, an arrangement of blocks, low walls, and ramps, all leading to a pool of blue and yellow blocks. I watch in amazement as a young man masterfully maneuvers through each of the obstacles, and then dives into the block pool.

"Are you kidding me?" A sudden frustrated voice behind me makes me jump, turning away from the obstacle course. Looking for the source of the noise, I scan the climbing walls. Atop the wall nearest me stands a tall, model-thin woman, pacing the length of the wall for a moment before descending, muttering a curse under her breath as she does. I'm torn between asking her if I can help with anything and walking away before she notices me. In my moment of hesitation, she sees me and shoots a glare in my direction.

"Is there a problem?" She puts her hands on her hips, the motion making her platinum-blonde hair bounce.

My face flushes. "Sorry," I say, slowly moving in her direction. "I was just gonna ask if you needed help."

The fire leaves the woman's gaze, and she gestures to the wall she just descended from. "My phone," she says. "I had it; I swear I had it before I climbed this wall, and now it's gone." She begins pacing back and forth again, her bony fingers tangling and untangling themselves between each other. Sweat beads on her forehead.

"Hey, don't worry about it," I tell her. "Just ask the front desk. Someone must have turned it in."

"I already asked Sasha," the young woman says, not looking in my direction. "She said no." The woman stops pacing, her eyelids sewn together tightly as she rubs her temples. "I'm trying to retrace my steps, but everything's...foggy."

Now, I've lost my phone before. Multiple times. I know how stressful it can be. But there's something about the way this woman is acting that gives me pause. It's like she didn't just lose an electronic device, but a literal lifeline. *Is that what I look like when I lose my phone?*

The strained expression drops from the woman's face, and she sighs. "What if she calls...?"

I want to ask who "she" is, but I decide not to pry. "I'll help you retrace your steps if you want," I tell her. "I've been in your shoes before."

She nods lightly. "Okay."

"I'm Crystal, by the way."

"Sadie," she says, still not looking at me, her hazel eyes fixed on the space between her shoes, the angry color in her cheeks gradually fading away. As if she notices me analyzing her expression, she suddenly looks up, forcing a smile as she looks at me. "Sorry, I didn't mean to drag you into my business. I'm just worried my daughter will call, and I'll miss it."

I hold up a hand. "Don't worry about it," I say. "It's my own fault. I'm ridiculously nosy, after all."

Sadie cracks a smile.

"We'll find your phone. Now, where's the last place you remember using it?"

* * *

After several torturous moments of watching Sadie rack her brain, she determined that the last place she used her phone was the women's locker room. We head in that direction, meticulously scanning each room and hallway we pass through. As we walk, I dial her number repeatedly, sifting through the muddled music overhead, trying to pick out a ringtone.

When we finally make it to the locker room, Sadie inhales deeply. "It's no use," she breathes. "I'm such an idiot."

"Don't worry." I click the "call" button again. "It'll turn up eventually."

Sadie shakes her head. "Not like she would have called anyway." She sinks onto a bench, hanging her head so that the bright blonde locks form a barrier around her face.

I sit down next to her, not sure what else to do. "How old is your daughter?"

"Nineteen. Her name's Lydia." After a moment, Sadie straightens up a bit, eyes glassy and staring off into the distance. "Just started college last year." Sadie's lip quivers. "I haven't spoken to her since..."

My chest tightens as the silence stretches on. This woman is a stranger, but her story kicks up complicated emotions like clouds of dust. I begin to feel sick to my stomach as I try not to think of my own parents.

"Lydia got taken from me," Sadie says at last. "I had issues...drugs, mostly." Her face crumples as though she is about to go down into a fit of sobbing, but she refuses to let the tears spill over. "When I got clean, and she graduated from high school, I started calling and calling. But she won't answer."

A chill washes over me, making the hairs on my arm stand on end. I'm caught up in this strange mixture of emotions. There's the natural discomfort of listening to a complete stranger's dark past. But part of me empathizes with this poor woman who just wants a relationship with her daughter—knows that everyone deserves a second chance.

There's a darker, more sinister voice undercutting this grace, though. A voice that says, *She had her chance. I wouldn't answer either. Anyone who loses their kid doesn't deserve their child's love.*

I bite my lip to keep from speaking because God knows what will come out.

"I just want her to know I've changed," Sadie continues. "Just want her to know I'm sorry. But who am I kidding?"

She stands, paces the floor of the locker room a few times. Rests against a locker door and drums her fingers against the metal.

"I'm sorry," I tell her, even though I only half mean it. "If I see your phone, I'll definitely turn it in."

She smiles, but it doesn't touch her eyes. "I'll be okay. Working out helps. Keeps my mind off things."

"Yeah." Her words flash me back to my conversation with Rory. Seems like everyone here uses exercise as a distraction from their own cruel realities. I'm in better company than I realized.

"I just need to...not think about her for a while. Y'know?"

"Yeah. I know."

* * *

Sadie decides to check the weight room for her phone one more time. I tag along, pondering our strange encounter. It's difficult not to make connections between her story and that of my estranged parents. I tell myself, it's not the same. I tell myself, my parents aren't sorry like Sadie seems to be. But then there's a nagging voice that assures me, I can't know that for sure—a sense of doubt that threatens to compromise the armor I'd worked so hard to construct over the years.

Dad did call, though. He did try. Right?

The thought bursts uninvited in my brain, and before I know it, my phone is in my hand, shaky fingers hovering over its surface.

Nope. I slide my phone back into my pocket. *I can't do it. Not today.*

So I decide to tag along with Sadie, patiently listening as she thinks out loud. It's better than the alternative, after all—better to listen to the woes of a stranger than to become consumed by my own. Despite knowing I've been in Mount Olympus for several hours, I stick close to Sadie as she does laps around the track to jog her memory. I'm getting a little tired, but the music sends an energizing jolt to my heart. A few more laps will help me shrug the heaviness off my soul, I'm sure.

I'm just about to break away from Sadie when an out-of-place smell catches my attention. Something faint but smoky. It catches me off guard, making me stop in my tracks.

"What's wrong?" Sadie asks.

I open my mouth to ask if she smells it too, but what I see when I look for the source of the odor makes my mouth hang open. A shaggy-haired elderly man crouches in one corner of the room. He nurses a cigarette, his dark eyes distant and disinterested. Despite being only a few feet away from me, he doesn't seem to notice that I'm gawking at him.

He doesn't belong. His clothes, his grubby appearance, his cigarette smell—it's like he wandered into Mount Olympus, thinking it was somewhere else, and then just decided to stay.

It's like he doesn't even know where he is.

"Hey!" Sadie waves a hand in front of my face, making me jump. "What's wrong?"

I point at the man. "Who's tha—?"

He's gone. The only evidence that he was ever here is the fading telltale scent of cigarette smoke.

Sadie cranes her head, facing the corner. "Who?"

I shudder, though I don't even know why. "Nothing. Forget it."

I can't stop staring at that corner, though. Part of me hopes that the man reappears. Part of me hopes he doesn't.

Mostly, I think I'm going crazy.

I think that's my cue to leave.

But when I say goodbye to Sadie and head toward the lobby, my feet drag. I sigh, the thought of being back in my apartment making me queasy.

I guess a few more laps won't kill me.

* * *

I'm about to step off the track and head home when I notice gym members trickling into the large exercise studio in the center of the walking track. My curiosity gets the better of me, and I follow one of them, peering through the glass door to see a large group gathering on mats around a muscular man with dark, shoulder-length dreadlocks. The class attendants stand on their mats, some of them stretching or doing yoga poses before the dreadlocked man stands and gestures for their attention.

I haven't done yoga in ages, but I enjoyed it the one time I did it. Trying not to catch anyone's attention, I push open the door and find an empty mat in the back while the dreadlocked man is going on about how this is a cell phone-free environment and asking everyone to put their phones in the basket outside. I had noticed the cell phone basket on my way in, but I am not an idiot; there's no way in hell I'm leaving my phone out there for someone else to steal. One man leaves the studio to follow the instructor's directive, but I simply slip my hand into my pocket and put the phone on silent mode.

When the rule-follower returns, the class begins. At first, it's just what I'd expect from a yoga session. I'm at least familiar with most of the poses, and I do my best, even though I'm not flexible enough to do all of them. The music in this room is different from that of the rest of the fitness center—calming, serene. The kind you'd expect to hear in a yoga center. I feel the tension from my restless night slide off me like shed skin.

Then the meditation session begins. That's where things get weird. Now, I did meditation last time I went to a yoga class, and it was well outside my comfort zone back then. Clearing my mind and focusing on the present has never been one of my strong points, after all.

This meditation is different, though. More intense.

There's nothing extraordinary about what the practitioner says. He tells us to visualize our ideal bodies, to really think about what that person looks like. Relaxed in the lotus position, I see an image of the Crystal Lunsford I would like to be: flattened stomach, reasonable breast size, skin free of acne scars, and the perpetual smile of someone happy with herself. As the yoga practitioner drones on, the visualization becomes more vivid, to the point where I sense that I'm right beneath her, a reverent disciple of this goddess of beauty.

The yoga practitioner's voice drifts in like a whisper of wind across a vast ocean: *"Visualize your goal, what is pushing you to pursue a healthier body."*

And just like that, the vision changes. Ideal Crystal crumples like a clay idol, replaced with a figure that makes my skin prickle with icy dread: Jace, his countenance twisted in a sneer. Jace, walking in slow motion toward our apartment door.

Jace, lying in the road, bleeding, his grotesque features illuminated by emergency lights that alternate between ghostly blue and hellish red.

My fault.

* * *

I emerge from the trance with some difficulty; it's like swimming from the bottom of a dark lake, leaving me cold and gasping for air. When I open my eyes, there's no one in the room other than the yoga instructor, who's kneeling over me and resting a hand on a clammy shoulder. He looks on in sympathy as tears slip down my burning cheeks, and I quickly wipe them away.

"You saw something that troubled you," he observes.

Fury lights up my chest, making me wrench my shoulder from his gentle grip. "What the hell kind of meditation was that?"

Dreadlocks is unperturbed by my accusation. "I can't control what you see in meditation," he explains. "Your demons are your own."

As much as that makes sense, something still feels *off*. What I'd experienced seemed closer to hypnosis than meditation. But then again, I don't know enough about either to be entirely sure one way or another.

I curl my knees to my chest as I wait for my breath to slow to a normal rate, for my heart to quit pounding in my head. The yoga instructor sits across from me and crosses his legs. For a long moment, he says nothing, and I am grateful. The last thing I want is to be compelled to share my traumatic vision with this stranger.

"The body and the mind are more connected than most people realize," he says at last. "Sometimes, improving the body helps to exorcise some of those demons in the mind. Perhaps you'll find the peace of mind you seek here."

With that, Dreadlocks stands and crosses the studio floor barefooted. He picks up a yellow-labeled bottle from a nearby shelf and tosses it to me. "I hope to see you again."

When he leaves, I lie on the mat and stare at the sky-blue ceiling, letting the bottle roll across the floor, away from me as I consider the yoga instructor's explanation.

Isn't yoga supposed to be relaxing? I think as I mentally replay the bizarre session. But then again, perhaps there was some truth to what Dreadlocks had said: *"Your demons are your own."*

Am I that far gone that I can't even allow myself to enjoy a moment's relaxation? Is my brain so broken that it has to morph something that should have brought me momentary peace into something horrifying?

Why am I still so hung up on someone who left me emotionally and psychologically scarred?

Why do I insist on blaming myself for his death?

Why can't I let go?

Chapter 6

Tonight, my sleep is infested with nightmares. Ugly dreams that linger in my mind throughout much of the morning after. At least I'm able to sleep, though; over the past year, sleep has been something of a luxury for me. And after the shadows of my nightmares slink away, I notice I'm feeling more energetic than I usually do. Normally, on a day like today, when cold air is oppressive like a wet blanket and the canopy of clouds echoes with threatening thunderclaps, all I'd want to do is curl up on the couch and watch TV. Today, though, there's something irresistible about the way the silver-tinged sunlight slices through my blinds. I want to get up. I want to move.

The weather app on my phone says that there's going to be a thunderstorm, though. So instead, I bounce around the apartment, trying to busy myself with whatever task I can get my hands on. I read, watch some TV, text Cici—who responds infrequently—and clean the house for the first time in months.

In the end, it's not enough, and I find myself flat on the couch, watching the ceiling fan blades rotate. I know what I want to do—I want to be back at Mount Olympus. But my experience with the weird yoga session keeps me from walking out the door even more than the projected storm does. Whenever I think of the deep trance I fell under and the images that flashed through my mind, my stomach lurches. Sure, I could just avoid yoga altogether, but then again...something about that session cast the whole fitness center in a bad light, and I'm not sure I'm ready to return to it.

My cell phone vibrates on the coffee table. Flipping over on my side, I see the screen lit up with a reminder: **Dr. Appt., 2:15 p.m.**

Immediately, I roll off the couch, nearly bumping my head against the corner of the coffee table in the process as I snatch up my phone again. *I can't believe I forgot!*

It's been weeks since I had follow-up blood work done, and I'm anxious to learn the results. A few months ago, I went to Dr. Vance about some gastrointestinal concerns, and after doing a blood test, he diagnosed me as pre-diabetic. He put me on a pill to lower my blood sugar and told me I need to change my lifestyle—more physical activity, less junk food.

I'm all in jitters as I lock the apartment door behind me and start toward the car. I'm replaying my progress over the last month in my head like I'm preparing for judgment day. I've been taking my meds somewhat recently, though sometimes I'm bad about remembering. I've been working out somewhat regularly. As for my diet... Well, I had kale once, so that should count for something.

For a moment, I consider rescheduling the appointment due to the bad weather, but I've already done that twice already. When I look out the window, I see no precipitation, so I tell myself not to worry, that the results have to be good. I may not have been perfect about following all the doctor's instructions, but the mere fact that I've tried must yield good results.

Right?

* * *

Wrong.

My heart drops when I step on the scale and the numbers blink three times before disappearing. I've actually *gained* weight—a little over two pounds—since my last visit to Dr. Vance. An indifferent nurse scribbles the damning numbers on her clipboard and ushers me into an empty waiting room, where Dr. Vance will soon enter and lecture me like an idiot child who isn't already painfully aware of the fact that she's fat.

I can't stand Dr. Vance. His bedside manner is nonexistent, and his arrogance shines through with every word that comes out of his thin-lipped mouth. I can't stand the way he talks down to me, and I really hoped I could avoid his disapproval today.

Should have just stayed on the couch.

There have been times when I've been left waiting for hours to be seen, but of course today Dr. Vance is right on time, knocking once on the door to signal his arrival before stepping in and sitting down at his computer, without so much as looking in my direction.

My leg bounces rapidly, and my fingers lace together, locking my hands onto my kneecap. Anxiety floods my mind, spilling into my chest and tightening it steadily with each passing silent second. Watching Dr. Vance type away on his computer, the screen reflected by his thick rectangular glasses, is unbearable. I'm tempted to leap to my feet and yell, *"Just tell me already!"*

"Crystal Lunsford," he says at last, still not looking at me. "You're here regarding blood test results?" He yawns.

"Yes," I say, fighting the swirling in the pit of my stomach.

"Well." He finally looks at me, his blue eyes burning into me like a merciless summer sky. "You certainly have a long way to go."

Thus begins the interrogation. Yes, I've been taking my meds. Yes, I've been working out. No, I haven't made any real diet changes because I have no self-control. Yes, I know that obesity is a huge risk factor in the United States. No, I don't want to get diabetes.

After volleying question after question at me, Dr. Vance removes his thick-rimmed glasses and shakes his head. The disappointment just drips off him, and I feel the distinctive urge to smack that smug look off his face. Who does he think he is, using that face—that face my stepmom used on me? The one Jace used on me.

"Crystal," he says, sitting up and fixing his eyes on the chart on his computer. "I don't think you understand the severity of your situation. You should think of yourself as one hamburger away from diabetes, from constantly living under the shadow of death's door."

I want to roll my eyes so hard, but I clench my jaw and resist the temptation. His dramatics are unbearable and the emotional manipulation, sickening.

And at the same time, I know he's right. Despite my snark and frustration, Dr. Vance has got me right where he wants me: terrified of my own body turning itself against me.

In the end, he increases my medication, which makes listening to his tired lecture about exercise and diet and that demon diabetes slightly more bearable. I thank him through gritted teeth and get out of that office as fast as possible, my medication script crumpled in my clenched fist.

In the pharmacy where I first met Rory, I scroll through the news app on my phone, trying to keep my self-sabotaging emotions at bay. Dr. Vance has left me feeling the way he always does: weak, low, wrong. The worst part is, there's truth in what he's said; I have to get my health under control somehow. I don't even think I can entirely justify my anger over his urgency.

But what he doesn't get is that *I can't do it.* I can't transform my body the way he and so many others have demanded over the years. It's too hard, and my mind gets in the way, chipping at any iota of self-determination I have within me. It's been like that since I was a teenager when my stepmom would get on my case.

I'm not strong enough.

So I sit here, waiting for my meds, half-reading about incoming tropical storms, celebrity gossip, and some new dance challenge that's going viral online.

Before long, I'm tired of reading and put my phone away, staring off into space. I'm not far from the aisle where Rory pitched Mount Olympus the other day. His words swim in my head, and I can't help but think about the talk he and I had had in the pool—how he'd spoken to me like a person, not fixating on my obvious obesity, but encouraging me in my journey toward a better body.

Why can't more people in my life be like him?

The pharmacist calls my name, holding up a little white paper bag. I collect the precious meds, swipe my debit card, and head for the door, still pondering Rory and Mount Olympus.

Before meeting Rory and taking his advice, I saw working out as a chore. Now, I actually find myself wanting to do it. Actually enjoying it. There is something magnetic about the environment of Mount Olympus.

Something addictive.

I wonder how much that has to do with Rory. I feel my cheeks flush at the thought, and I switch on the car, letting the AC pump cool air in.

There are five days left in my suspension. Five days to get a jump start on my workout routine and get my diet in order. Five days to get the momentum I need to push me through this perpetual rut.

Five days to get to know Rory.

At that moment, I decide to really commit. I've "committed" to workout routines and diet fads before but to no avail. But something inside me has shifted. I can feel it.

This time will be different.

Chapter 7

Breezing through those glass double doors is like a breath of fresh air the following day. I haul my overstuffed workout bag across the mist-covered concrete and am surprised to see Sasha working reception again. She's examining her teeth in a little pocket mirror, and when the doors shut behind me, she gets that look on her face that suggests I'm her best friend she hasn't seen in ages.

"You're back!" she pipes up from behind her desk. "Where've you been, Crystal?"

Reaching the reception desk, I drop the duffel bag to the floor and take a deep breath. "Been busy. Had to do some thinking." I rifle through my purse and retrieve my wallet. "I decided I need to get a membership."

Sasha's already wide smile lengthens to the point where I'd think it'll split her face. Instantly, she opens a drawer and whips out a packet of paper, overlaying a few signature lines with a green highlighter. "Sign here, here, here, aaaand...here!"

While I'm inscribing the packets with my ugly signature, Sasha repeats what she said the other day about the discounts and my payment plan. I do my best to tune her out, focusing again on the task set before me. Part of me wants to meticulously read, or at least skim, the document for unacceptable terms and conditions, but I know myself: if I start reading the thing, I'll reconsider joining Mount Olympus altogether. *Just bite the bullet*, I tell myself.

Before the ink on my last signature is dry, I slide the packet across the desk. Sasha examines it hastily, then snatches my hand up in a firm handshake. "So that makes it official, darlin'," Sasha says. "Welcome to Mount Olympus!"

* * *

I should feel good, having made such an investment in my health. But as I emerge from the navy-blue reception into the bright-walled corridor leading to the weight room, I can't help but feel a sense of foreboding resulting from my decision. Sure, Sasha seems nice enough, and I can't deny that this is an excellent fitness center, one that I can actually see myself going to regularly and enjoying.

But $90 a month is still a big deal. I know it's doable, but part of me wishes I hadn't signed that contract quite so quickly.

In my pondering, I nearly collide with Clarissa the free sample lady—again. She rounds the corner and gasps but notices me just in time to avoid spilling her plastic cups.

"You again!" she says, a mischievous smile on her face. "I swear, you're trying to kill me."

I hold up my hands. "I swear, I'm not. Just klutzy."

"Right," she says with mock suspicion. "Well, could I offer you some Ambrosia to bolster you in your assassination attempt?"

My first instinct is to refuse like last time, but the moment of brief humor we've shared makes me more inclined to learn more. "What even *is* Ambrosia?" I ask. "You probably told me, but I forgot."

Her face lights up, and I know I'm in for a hell of a pitch. I sort of wish then that I hadn't asked, but I lean up against the wall and prepare to listen patiently.

"Essentially, Ambrosia is a combination between a sports drink and an energy drink. The best of both worlds. It doesn't merely replenish nutrients your body has lost during strenuous exercise—it gives you the energy to push yourself."

"Okay," I say, pondering her description. As I'm listening, I can't shake the idea that a sports/energy drink is a terrible idea, the kind of thing that would be banned by the FDA not long after its inception.

"Beginners find themselves able to run for miles after drinking this stuff. Even advanced fitness buffs surprise themselves with what they're able to do." She takes a step closer to me, so the tray is directly beneath me; looking down, I see my pudgy face reflected in the little liquid-filled cups. "You see, your body is more capable than you give it credit for. Ambrosia just gives you that little 'push' to take your workout from good to great. Not only that, but you'll find yourself enjoying yourself more."

As Clarissa finishes her pitch, I feel my suspicion steadily die down as I consider the alleged benefits of this concoction. If there's been one problem with my experience working out, it's that I hate it. Sure, there's that brief surge of endorphins that everyone talks about, but in my experience, that's overrated. It's not enough to make me want to keep working out.

I think of Dr. Vance and the mocking teenagers at the restaurant. I think of Jace and my stepmother, their criticism and cruelty over my weight. I can't bear that kind of ridicule anymore, and if I'm going to reach my goal, I'll need all the help I can get.

When I lift up one of the little cups, Clarissa's eyes follow my motions, bright and eager to gauge my reaction. When I down the sample, the first thing that hits me is the taste, cool and sweet at first like citrus but then tangy—almost spicy—like cayenne, making my taste buds dance. An exhilarating sensation propels throughout my body, waking up every sleeping nerve electrically charging every cell. My muscles hum with energy.

For the first time in over a year, I feel *alive*.

Clarissa chuckles. "Good, right?"

The wildness courses through my veins in waves, making me tremble.

Good? Good doesn't even begin to cover it.

Clarissa gives me a knowing grin. "If you want more, there are samples all throughout the building."

"Awesome! Thanks."

I turn on one heel and jog toward the weight room.

* * *

What follows next is nothing short of a spiritual experience.

I jump on the elliptical and pump my limbs vigorously until the digital hourglass blinks away, hardly slowing down. Far from exhausted after that, I'm compelled to release the energy that has turned my blood to liquid lightning.

I'm not a runner, but my legs want to run, run, run. I tell myself I can't do it, that I've done enough work already, but this pressure builds in me, making me feel agitated and restless.

Run, run, run, run, goes my heartbeat.

So, jumping off the elliptical, I head upstairs to the walking track that overlooks the weight rooms and the basketball courts. I walk, then jog, but it's not taking the edge off. I'm wired as hell, and my blood is lightning, and my heartbeat goes, *Run! Run! Run! Run!* So I push myself harder and harder, and before I know it, I'm sprinting down the track, passing jogger after jogger so quickly that they're nothing but blurred colors in my peripheral vision.

I might as well be flying.

It seems impossible, but I'm enjoying myself. As long as I keep my body moving, I'm happier than I've felt in ages. And I see no reason to slow down. Somehow, I'm unburdened by aching legs and wheezing lungs and my constant companion, exhaustion. It's as though I've been reincarnated as a true athlete. A warrior. A goddess.

At least, that's what it feels like. I know my form is terrible and that flab is bouncing all over the place. I avoid my reflection as I pass the mirrors along the edge of the track, where the ugly truth threatens to ruin my moment. I'm so high on feeling alive that, for the first time in a long time, I don't care how I look. I just want to keep feeling strong. Just a little while longer.

I keep waiting for the high to die down. I slow my pace when a funny feeling makes my stomach twist up because there's something wrong about feeling this good during a workout, especially one this long. I should be tired by now.

It pains me to think about going home, but I know can't stay here forever. Pulling my phone out of my pocket, I gasp when I realize I've lost over three hours here! Slowing to a brisk walk, I steer myself off the walking track and toward the stairwell. I'm about to pull out my phone to check the time when I see another tray of cups of Ambrosia. My heart races. I'm reaching out to grab one of the tiny Styrofoam cups, but my mind is screaming, *Go home already!* even as my heartbeat pumps out, *Run, run, run, run* with equal urgency.

"You done already?" a male voice asks from beside me.

I jump, my head whipping around to see a yellow-clad custodian with smoke-colored eyes, leaning on a mop handle and looking at me with amusement.

"Yeah. I've got some stuff to get done." I snap up one of the cups and down the Ambrosia in one chug.

And there it is again. That sensation like molten lightning sizzling throughout my whole body. The custodian is going on about how he wishes he could be working out instead of mopping this floor, but I'm not even half listening.

I'm explosive. My soul is fighting to charge out of my body, and I'm going to have to run like mad to recover it. Goosebumps make my flesh rise, and my hands shake as I resist the urge to run in a hundred different directions at once.

The custodian waves his hand over my eyes. "Hello?"

I blink and shake my head, attempting to refocus on him. I will my twitchy hands to remain steady. "Sorry. Lost in thought."

He shrugs. "All I asked was if you'd seen the pool yet."

I nod, silent as my mind and my body do battle once again. It's useless, though; no sooner than the word "pool" is uttered do my feet rush off in the direction of the aquatics room.

Before I know it, I'm swimming in the Olympic-sized pool. I've never been the greatest swimmer, but I know how to do a decent enough crawl stroke, at least. The rush of endorphins from my last shot of Ambrosia is still in full effect, enabling me to complete lap after lap without tiring out. It doesn't take long for me to build up my confidence, and soon, I'm racing against the huge timer on the wall.

That's when I realize something strange: there's a timer but no clocks in this room. I slow my pace and hang off the pool wall, letting my feet dangle idly in the water as the reality sinks in—I haven't seen a clock *anywhere* in Mount Olympus.

Something about that thought makes me uneasy, and as I rest against the pool wall, I try to estimate how long I've been here since I left my phone in the locker room. The harder I try, the more difficult it is to think about it. The effort results in a wave of dizziness that makes the world tilt, so I clamber out of the pool so fast that I slip and hit the cold tile floor on my side, nearly knocking my head against the diving block.

The lifeguard rushes toward me in an instant, blowing his whistle and toting his big red rescue tube. "You okay?" he asks, scanning my body for injuries.

I nod. "I'm fine," I say, but I let him help me up when he extends his hand.

"You've really been pushing it," he says, sounding equally concerned and impressed. "Wish I had that kind of energy. You must be tired."

I shake my head, though I know that, by now, I should be beyond tired. "Just thirsty," I tell him. And the moment the words come out of my mouth, I realize how true they are. My throat is dry, and my tongue is like a sun-dried sponge sitting in my mouth. How can that be? It seems like I've done nothing but drink liquids since I got here.

"Wait here," the lifeguard says, straightening up and walking over to a cooler by the lifeguard stand. He produces a yellow-labeled bottle of clear liquid and offers it to me.

I don't hesitate, ripping off the cap and swallowing greedily, downing the Ambrosia in a matter of seconds.

Any concerns I had earlier simply blink out of existence. I toss aside the empty bottle and dive back into the pool, pumping my arms and legs to the beat of the muddled music blasting overhead.

I should be tired by now.

Why am I not tired?

* * *

In the locker room, I lie on a bench, staring at the ceiling as I wait for the Ambrosia-induced high to finally taper off. I clench and unclench my fists. My legs twitch as waves of chills ripple throughout my body, making my skin rise with goosebumps. I'm keenly aware of the thundering heartbeat in my chest, and with eyes sewn shut, I try to coach the various systems in my body working on overdrive to slow down. Breathe.

Just when I think I'm starting to calm down, the screech of a screen door yanks me out of my meditation. I whip my head upward so fast that I nearly topple off the bench, then look up to see Sadie saunter into the locker room. She's about to pass me without a word, but I raise a hand in greeting. "Hey, Sadie," I say.

She turns to face me, her eyes wide and wild. Then her brow crinkles in an expression I easily recognize: she knows she knows me, but she can't remember my name.

I help her out. "Crystal. We met the other day, looking for your phone."

Sadie's expression changes from confusion to relief to bewildered disappointment all in the space of five seconds. "Right," she says, eyes glassy and unfocused.

"Did you ever find it?" Even as I extract details of that day from my memory, it feels further away than it should.

"Find what?" At first, I think she's joking. She must be. But the lost look on her face shows me she's sincere.

"...Your phone. Did you find it?"

A pause. Her sweaty brow crinkles as she considers my question way longer than necessary. "...No." Even as she answers, she doesn't seem certain. It's as though her own response doesn't make sense to her.

I want to ask her more questions, but the stupor she's in makes the words die in my throat. I can almost hear the gears in her head grinding slowly as she readjusts to the minor interruption I placed in her routine. As I ponder why she looks so off, I remember another detail from my conversation with her.

"Are you okay?" I ask at last, voice shaking. "Did something happen with...your daughter?"

Now her eyes narrow, glaring at me. I feel my entire body tense up, unsure of what I've done wrong but preparing to defend myself against her retaliation nonetheless. When her clammy hands ball up into fists, I slide off the bench and back up toward the wall of lockers, holding my hands up defensively.

But just when I think she's about to go off on me, she shifts her glare to a point to the left of me. Without even looking at me, she strides across the floor, opens a locker, and produces a yellow-labeled bottle with a clear liquid inside: Ambrosia. She tosses back the contents of the bottle without stopping for a breath, and when she's finished, the change in her countenance is nearly instantaneous. The confused aggression slides off her, and her face lights up as though she's swallowed sunshine itself.

"A-are you okay?" The words sound faint and weak to my own ears. Slamming her locker door shut, she smiles at me, dropping the Ambrosia bottle on the floor in front of me. As she jogs out of the locker room, I pick up the empty bottle and stare at it, pondering the change in Sadie that occurred in a mere forty-eight-hour span. That couldn't have been the same person, I tell myself. She can't have been.

I consider the possibilities. Something must have happened. Maybe she got bad news from her daughter. Maybe she's caught up in other family drama. Maybe the Sadie I spoke to so briefly had another, less genial side.

Or maybe... I fidget with the Ambrosia bottle in my hand, remembering how it seemed to hijack my own brain mere minutes ago. Could a sports drink really make someone act that way?

But the longer I peer into the empty bottle, the more hollow I feel inside. Thirst makes my chest ache and my stomach swirl.

Just a little more, I decide, dropping the bottle in a recycling bin as I exit the locker room. One more workout, then home.

Home. It's funny how that one word makes my heart sink.

Chapter 8

Of course, I don't leave. I try, though. I even make it as far as the entrance to the lobby once. But Clarissa stops me with those free samples of Ambrosia, and it's then that I notice how tiny the cups are and that I'll need *at least* three if I'm going to be able to tackle the climbing walls.

So I stay a little longer.

I don't check the time on my phone as often as I used to. Don't really see the need to. It seems like time has slowed down—I can do laps in the pool, race up and down the climbing walls, and run a few miles on the treadmill, all within half an hour.

It shouldn't be possible. I stare at the digits on the screen, chills rocketing up my back as I try to make sense of what I'm seeing. As I pocket the phone, I start walking toward the lobby. Time doesn't just slow down. But maybe...I've just gotten faster?

The idea doesn't seem as silly as it probably should. I mean, the Ambrosia certainly has affected me, enabling me to do more than I ever thought I could. It must be the reason I'm able to power through exercises at such an alarming speed.

I'm back in the lobby, staring at the exit door as I've done time and time again. The light filtering through the door is just as unchanged as it was before. Deep within my soul, I can sense the wrongness. I've been here too long, I tell myself. It's been... My head instantly begins to hurt when I try to calculate my time in Mount Olympus.

So I stop trying. *I can't leave yet*, I tell myself, turning away from the lobby. *The sooner I leave, the sooner I'll crawl back to my disgusting, fat-pig habits.*

Mount Olympus is my sanctuary until I carve this loathsome body into what I need it to be.

It's not like I'm missing anything at home. I inhale deeply, pushing aside my gnawing suspicions. *It's not like anyone's missing me.*

* * *

The next several hours—or has it been days?—are like something out of a trance or a pleasant dream. I keep myself in a state of perpetual motion, exploring Mount Olympus and pushing myself with its many amenities.

No matter how hard I work, though, I'm never satisfied. There's this feeling in my chest like an itch that always needs to be scratched, and it's bearable as long as I keep on moving, moving, moving.

I'm a bomb on the verge of eruption, and constant movement is the only thing that keeps my body from exploding into millions of pieces.

So I keep moving, driven by that unquenchable thirst for the Ambrosia. The more I drink, the more I want. And when I'm not drinking it, I crave it. The delicious sweetness. The spicy aftertaste that sets my bloodstream on fire. My hands tremble with the need to hold another cup, but I will them to hold the handles of the stationary bike I'm on instead.

I'm caught in a cycle: *Drink, move, drink, move...*

Drink. Out of the corner of my eye, I catch a glimpse of the front door, where the sun is shining. It looks to be somewhere around noon. Have I been here all night? Has it been more than one night since I was supposed to leave? What about work? I shut my eyes and try to remember how many days of my suspension I have left. I reach for my phone to check the time. Before I can produce it, a staff member saunters up to me and shoves me a water bottle with the Mount Olympus logo on it, congratulating me on my new membership. Without hesitating, I take a sip from the bottle. The Ambrosia wakes up my taste buds, setting my neurons on fire.

Move. Attached to the stationary bike is a huge flatscreen displaying a digital forest spread out before me. Light filters through the leaves of the towering trees, and I feel a twinge of nostalgia. Vaguely, I remember playing in the woods behind my family's house as a child. My heart races at the memory, and I peel my sweat-soaked body off the bike, abandoning the recollection in the digital forest and heading toward the front lobby. My mind screams that something is wrong here. But the fear and the yearning for home vanishes when I...

Drink. Clarissa and her tray catch me as they always do. She's got that saccharine smile on her face as I down cup after cup of Ambrosia, not even minding as I let the plastic cups litter the floor. I stand there in front of her, taking deep breaths until I feel okay again. The anxiety that has crept up within me vanishes, replaced by pure energy. I turn my back on Clarissa and head toward the weight room again.

Move. I'm surrounded by buff guys and girls, the type who always intimidated me before I started at Mount Olympus. I'm bench pressing fifty pounds, then seventy pounds. The more I push myself, the more pride swells within me. But then I look around and re-examine the other people in the weight room. Sure, there are true athletes in the room, but there are also people who look just like me. People who shouldn't be able to lift as much as they are. But they are, and with very little effort. The element of challenge is nowhere to be found.

A familiar feeling of wrongness makes my stomach twist up. I sit on the bench press machine and put my head in my hands. And there it is again, that taunting question: *How long have I been here?*

And then I notice it again: that smoky cigarette smell wafting from one corner of the room. I sense the old man's presence before I see him, shaggy and shabby as ever, casually blowing cigarette smoke in the air. When a twiggy gym patron jogs past him—mere inches away from his outstretched legs—he doesn't even look up to acknowledge her presence. She runs on, seemingly oblivious to his presence.

But how? The sight of this harmless old man sets off alarm bells in my mind. I can't reconcile his existence in this place. All I can do is stare.

"Well, fancy seeing you here!"

Craning my neck around, I see Rory leaning up against the wall across from me, his arms crossed and that look of boyish mischief on his face. Seeing him soothes me momentarily, but when I turn back around to see that the old man has once again disappeared, I swallow hard. I think about asking him if he saw the guy too, but remembering Sadie's reaction keeps me from bothering. Instead, I manage a weak smile, letting Rory's comforting presence gradually put my suspicions to rest. For now.

"Didn't know you could bench press like that." Rory raises a golden eyebrow, his admiration evident in that cute half-smile.

I release a nervous laugh. "Neither did I."

Stuffing his hands in the pockets of his basketball shorts, he strides toward me. "So, I take it you're feeling the effects of Mount Olympus's worst-kept secret." He leans against the weight machine and looks down at me.

"It's like..." I begin, fumbling for the right words. "I shouldn't be *able* to do all this. I'm never tired. Never hungry. It's like...I'm barely even human."

Rory blinks, waiting for me to continue.

"But as wrong as that is, part of me doesn't even care. It's exhilarating, pushing my body this way, and I want…" A distant memory threatens to corrupt my thoughts, and I push it back down. "I want a perfect body, no matter what it takes."

Rory nods. "Yep, that's the Ambrosia talking," he says. "The thing is, though, you were just as capable before you started it as you are now. Ambrosia just helps you laser-focus on your goal. It shuts off the senses that would otherwise get in the way. Mind over matter, and all."

He meant to encourage me with that statement, but now I'm uneasy again. Do I really want my senses "shut off"?

Straightening up, Rory says, "Well, I've got to get a move on. It's almost time for my class."

"Your class?" I smile, standing to meet his eyes. "I didn't know you worked here too."

"Just started." Rory starts walking toward the stairs, and I find myself following. "I pitched the idea to management, and they thought it was a great idea."

"What kind of class is it?" A faint memory of my strange experience at yoga class pops into my head, and I instinctively slow my steps.

"Well…maybe 'class' isn't an accurate term."

* * *

Rory leads me to the yoga studio, which has been transformed into a nightclub. He is poised behind a DJ's turntable in one corner of the room where a large group of people dance wildly under the flashing lights. I smile as Rory leads the "class." No instructions, no rules. Just fun.

I'm not much of a dancer, though, so I'm content standing by the door and observing. That is until DJ Rory calls me out.

"Ladies and gentlemen, we have a special guest here with us." He gestures dramatically toward me, making my cheeks burn. "A brand-new member of Mount Olympus, joining us from Little Rock, give it up for Crystal Lunsford!"

I know he did not *just do that,* I think, glaring at Rory from across the room. The "nightclub" erupts into applause, and soon, sweaty arms are reaching out, beckoning me to join them. Rory winks at me from behind the DJ table, and I shake my head at him, mouthing *"Hell, no."* No way am I making a fool of myself in front of all these people.

The herd of dancers hovers closer to me, threatening to absorb me within itself. I stand stubbornly firm—until one girl shoves a yellow-labeled bottle in my face. She smiles almost drunkenly, wrapping an arm around my shoulders and waiting for me to take the bottle from her.

No, not again... I know exactly where this is going to lead.

But at the same time, my dry lips quiver with that sudden, familiar thirst. My taste buds remember how the Ambrosia felt on my tongue, and it doesn't take long for me to reach up and snatch the bottle from the intrusive stranger.

And within seconds of downing the bottle's contents, I'm ready to party.

The dancers watching the exchange all holler when I spike the bottle onto the dance floor like a football player celebrating at the endzone. I shout along with them and let the girl guide me into the center of the horde. The music seems louder now, faster, and I'm jumping and flailing around mindlessly, not caring in the slightest how I look, partially because I know most everyone here looks just as foolish as I probably do.

Caught up in this wild electric frenzy, I savor that pleasant sensation of my mind shutting down. My prior inhibitions, shutting down. My soul, a slave to my body and its insatiable desire. There's no fear, no insecurity—not when my heartbeat and the bass-heavy club music are so perfectly synchronized.

Move! Move! Move! Move!

* * *

The party lingers on until finally Rory switches off the black lights and turns on the fluorescents, transforming the nightclub back into a yoga studio. Turning off and packing up his DJ equipment, he casts a warm glance toward me. I jog toward him, still feeling the effects of the Ambrosia but to a lesser extent than earlier.

"Incredible, right?" Rory says.

"Incredible," I echo. "When is the next class...party? Whatever you call it?"

He grins. "Just listen for the music, and come running."

It's a strange, unhelpful answer, but somehow, it's enough. "You know I will."

His gray eyes drift away from my face and toward my stomach. I feel uneasy until he finally says, "You're losing weight, you know."

My eyes widen, as if I'm not sure that I heard him correctly. When was the last time that anyone had said those words to me? Has it *ever* happened?

"It looks good on you."

I beam with pride, my eyes watering unexpectedly. "Thanks, Rory."

With that, he gives me one last little smile, picking up his DJ equipment and heading toward the studio door. "See ya around."

My stomach somersaults as I process Rory's compliment. It's strange: Despite having worked out so much, I hadn't checked my weight in...how long?

How long?

Wait.

How long have I been here?

I reach for my cell phone to check the time, but when I stick my hand in the pocket of my leggings, all I find is a tube of lip balm.

My phone is gone.

Instantly, my euphoria is replaced by panic. I scan the floor of the yoga studio/dance floor, thinking that maybe it simply slipped out during the dance party. There's nothing, though.

Shit.

I step out into the hall and try to retrace my steps. Where's the last place I used it? I think it was downstairs in front of the weight room, but no. I hadn't actually touched my phone; just thought about it. Did I use it anywhere else? Have I gotten any calls or texts? Has my phone even rung? No, I had it on silent. Right? But when did I do that? And why?

Then I vaguely remember my argument with Dad from the other day. Pain ricochets in my head as I try to recall the details. I inhale sharply, stumbling aside and placing a hand against the wall to steady myself. My temple throbs, blurring my vision for a second, and I try to blink it away. I inhale deeply, calmly, and the pain dulls to a soft ache.

I go to the front desk and approach Sasha, who I'm no longer surprised is still working after all this time—maybe she lives here. She's tapping away on her computer with those perfect nails when I step up to her desk and clear my throat.

"Well, hey there!" she says brightly as if greeting an old friend after a long time. "You've enjoyed your visit, I take it?"

I nod and manage a smile. Out of the corner of my eye, I see Clarissa and her tray. My skin becomes clammy and my hands begin to sweat, but I fight to focus on Sasha. "It's been good, but—"

"You're not leaving already." Her lips curve into a pouty frown. "Are you?"

"No!" I abruptly say, surprising myself. The ache in my head intensifies as I try to ignore the screaming voice in my head that insists that I should, in fact, be leaving. "I lost my phone. I was wondering if someone had turned one in."

"Let me check the lost and found," she says, stepping away from the desk and into a back room. As I wait for her, I look around and notice an unsettling emptiness permeating the lobby. The gym proper is abuzz with activity, but with Sasha's absence, I'm completely alone. Well, other than Clarissa, whose presence is like that of an apparition at the back of the room. My mouth waters, and I grip the edge of Sasha's desk hard as if it's the only thing keeping me from flying across the room to the source of my temptation.

At last, Sasha returns with that same pouty look on her face. "Couldn't find anything, hon. No phones have been turned in."

My heart goes cold, seems to stop beating altogether as I process the news. It's just a phone, but it feels more than that. Even though Sasha is right across from me, somehow, I feel even more alone than before.

I think about asking Sasha how long I've been here. If I really want to know, all I have to do is ask.

If I really want to know...

I need to leave. The exit is so very close. Cell phones can be replaced.

I don't have to stay here, I tell myself, glancing toward the exit door. *I can leave... if I really want to.*

But I make the mistake of turning around—of facing Clarissa. Clarissa waves at me, and my flesh begins to crawl as I fight to keep a hold of the overwhelming desire. It's useless, though. Thirst, even more powerful than what I've felt before, hits me, making my body hollow and empty. I drift toward Clarissa as if being pulled by an invisible thread.

"Hello again!" she chirps as I approach her, but I don't respond. Instead, I pick up one cup after another and toss back their intoxicating contents. The familiar taste seems to revive the hollow, parched places in my body. But I don't stop there, taking cup after cup as the lightning-bolt sensation radiates from my head throughout my entire body. My vision blurs, replaced by blinding white, a light that burns brighter and brighter until it drowns out all sound and sense. And even then, I can't stop, not until I've emptied the last cup.

Gradually, the whiteness fades. My vision sharpens, and I feel a trickle of Ambrosia slide down my chin. Wiping it away, I see the empty cups on the floor and on Clarissa's tray. The sight triggers a memory of my apartment floor, littered with take-out boxes and candy wrappers—the ugly evidence of my binging, or "sadness eating" as I had called it back then. Night after lonely night of eating to dull the pain and the shame over what happened to Jace, only to be overwhelmed by even more shame.

"Fat pig, fat pig..."

I look down at Clarissa, preparing for the inevitable look of disgust over my act of gluttony. But it never comes. Instead, she's smiling that free and easy smile that I've grown accustomed to seeing from her. She almost looks pleased with me.

"Enjoy your workout!" Clarissa says, gesturing toward the weight room.

I quickly take off in that direction, my movements mechanical. My body knows what it craves, but deep in my mind, fear like a spreading flame begins to take root. As I jump on the elliptical for the umpteenth time, I pump my limbs as hard as I can as the pieces click together in my endorphin-charged mind.

Despite the euphoria that helps me complete stride after stride on the machine, despite the upbeat music that fills the air, a shadow of suspicion is lodged in my brain like a pebble in my shoe—enough to cause some discomfort.

But not enough.

Chapter 9

I don't return to Sasha. Sometimes I wonder if anyone has turned in my cell phone, but not enough to tear myself away from my exercise. It's like the moment I slide out of the pool or step off a workout machine, I'm hit with this intense wave of guilt and self-disgust. Because there are no excuses in Mount Olympus. No "too tired" or "too hungry" or "too much in pain." A cup of Ambrosia is all it takes to make any ill effects vanish.

There are flickers now and again—brief moments when I come to my senses and nearly walk out the door. A sight or smell sometimes triggers a memory of someone I've left behind—my family, a coworker, Jace.

I endure these flickers as one endures a bout of nausea; they're uncomfortable but easily remedied. Again, one shot of Ambrosia is all it takes to make the bad thoughts and the worries go away. One shot, and that sensation like a million little lightning bolts brings me to that state of ecstasy, one in which I transcend my petty human past. I'm never unhappy as long as I *move, move, move, move.*

I've never been high before. I wonder if this was what it's like.

Everything's good. That is until I look in the mirror and get hung up on some detail that anchors me to the outside world.

I'm in the women's locker room after racing—and nearly beating—the guy in the lane next to me in an impromptu swimming race. The locker room is empty, save one woman taking a lengthy shower on the other end of the room, so I take plenty of time to admire myself in the mirror.

Rory was right... I have lost weight! I smile, realizing how not too long ago, my stomach had bulged over the top of my leggings. Now, I'm noticing the change, the way my stomach has flattened. I run my hand over the skin, marveling at my transformation.

But then, while I'm toweling myself off, I notice something small and silver caught in the thick fabric, an object whose shape feels vaguely familiar.

My wrinkled fingers fumble with the thing—a little cross attached to a chain around my neck—and release it from the white threads that ensnare it.

I hold it in my palm and give it a long stare, my clouded mind straining to figure out its significance. I fold my hand over it, pressing hard until its edges poke my skin.

In that moment, it transforms from a simple object to a memory-triggering talisman. I vaguely remember this feeling, the softness of the colors and shapes forming behind my closed eyes. I remember resisting, pushing the memories down to the back of my mind. But I don't remember why. So I brace myself, grip the necklace like life itself, and let myself remember.

The night before my tenth birthday. Months before, my parents had split, and my sleep was plagued by nightmares. Waking up, I call out for Mom.

But wait. Mom's not here.

And she won't be here tomorrow for my birthday party.

My dad hears me crying and gently knocks on the door, walks over, and kneels beside my bed. I tell him how scared and sad I am. He leaves for a few seconds, then comes back with a silver necklace. An early birthday present to chase away the nightmares and anxiety. Clasping it around my neck, he whispers words of comfort.

I stumble backward, taken aback by the force of the vision. It wasn't a suppressed memory. Just an abandoned one, one that I tried not to dwell on if I could help it. But somehow, I'm mentally exhausted from conjuring that image of one of my last tender moments with my father, before everything went wrong. Producing the memory has put a great deal of strain on my mind, like I've been drawing water from the depths of a well.

I had buried such an important memory so easily.

What else have I forgotten?

And then another thought occurs to me, compelling me to glance at myself in the mirror once again. The weight loss...I'm still overweight, but the change is noticeable. This sort of change doesn't happen overnight, much less in a few hours.

And I've only been here a few hours... right?

How long have I been here?!

Still dressed in my bathing suit, I run into the corridor that connects the pool to the main lobby. I peer through the window to the pool and force myself to see what I haven't wanted to notice before.

The light coming through the outside windows hasn't changed since my arrival here—it's just as cloudy and dismal as it was before, and night hasn't fallen in all this time.

I look at the swimmers—really look at them. Half of them look just as I expect them to—frantic and frenzied as they cut through the water, high off Ambrosia like I am. The other half...something seems off about them.

They move too slowly, too fluid in their movements. Almost robotic. Almost inhuman.

My eyes drift toward the lifeguard stand. I remember the scruffy-haired lifeguard from earlier when I fell. But no...after all this time, he should have been replaced by another worker. Why is he still here?

Why am *I* still here?

I take off toward the lobby, determined to make it home.

I'm not paying attention to where I'm going and end up running headlong into Clarissa again, nearly knocking her cups of Ambrosia to the floor.

I hesitate. My muddled mind still vaguely remembers my last encounter with Clarissa, how greedily I emptied all the cups on her free sample tray. How quickly I fell back into the cycle of *drink, move, drink, move.*

She's looking at me with that cool smile of hers. It's like she knows I'm not strong enough to resist. Not today. Even though the thirst is overwhelming, and even though my feet drag like lead as I step away from her, I call over my shoulder, "I'm leaving!"

Clarissa nods, still grinning—no, not grinning. Smirking. The calculated way she's looking at me makes my skin crawl, so I keep my eyes on the front door.

I see Sasha out of the corner of my eye and can almost hear the pout in her voice as she asks me, "Are you leaving already?"

Hell yeah, I'm leaving. I set my jaw and set my gaze firmly on the exit door. Just a few more steps.

But the closer I get to the door, the heavier my legs seem to get. By the time I actually reach the door, I feel something I haven't felt since I started drinking Ambrosia: real exhaustion. It's as though my body is just now realizing that, oh yeah, it actually needs sleep, food, rest— things that I've neglected in my time at Mount Olympus.

I reach out to clutch the door handle, and my knees buckle. My overexerted muscles burn with agony, and I crumble to the floor, lying on my side and peering through the door window to the bleary outside world. Searing pain rockets up and down my shins, and I try to stand up again, but I'm too weak.

Too weak.

Too fat.

Too disgusting.

The bad thoughts creep back in like unwelcome shadows in this endless day. I grit my teeth as the pain makes my muscles throb, and I hear Jace's voice in my head saying, *"Fat pig. Fat pig."*

Clarissa appears by my side. Her smile seems more sympathetic than smug as she holds out one of her free sample cups. "When was the last time you had something to drink? You're probably dehydrated."

No. No, that's not it.

There's something wrong with that drink. I can't drink it. But dammit, I hate this weakness. I hate this weight and ache in my chest, and I know that stupid cup will take it all away. And I want it gone. I don't just want Ambrosia—I can't survive without it. I don't know how I survived beyond the walls of Mount Olympus this last year.

Self-loathing and helplessness flood me.

A tear slides down my cheek as I reach out to take the drink from her. I toss it back, and the knots untangle in my chest. The fog of despair fades, chased away by relief and a strength that revives me in a way only Ambrosia can.

Miraculously cured of the moment of weakness and pain, I get up and back a few feet away from the front door. I can't go out there. Ambrosia makes me stronger than I could ever hope to be—and it can only be found here, within these walls.

By the time I'm jogging toward the walking track, my suspicions have vanished, along with any desire I'd had for freedom.

After all, I'm already free.

Chapter 10

I'm so damn happy.

In the pool, on the treadmill, on the track, on the climbing walls. So very happy as I keep moving, moving, moving. Never stopping, never resting, never dwelling on the faceless visions of the people and places who used to take up too much space in my life.

I'm in an intense tennis match with another girl when, for half a second, I worry that I'm missing my shift at work.

I'm ascending the diving board, trying to remember where I work.

I'm doing sit-ups in the weight room, and I'm unemployed.

With every sip of Ambrosia and every resulting workout session, I'm losing my memories. I can feel it, like heavy weights sliding out of my skull, leaving behind a comfortable emptiness.

I'm forgetting Jace.

Yes, Jace, the man who had haunted me from beyond the grave.

The longer I stay here, the more his memory fades. I'm floating on my back in the therapy pool when I feel that familiar fist constricting my heart slowly, gently releasing its grip when the remnants of his memory slide into my subconscious.

He's gone. At last, he's gone.

Just like that, I'm free. A smile climbs up my face as I flip onto my stomach and do a few somersaults in the saltwater pool, relishing in the death of a trauma I can't even remember.

* * *

Drink. Move. Drink. Move. It's easier now than ever before to fall in line with the heartbeat of Mount Olympus. I ride every Ambrosia-induced high as long as it will take me, and when I come down, I jump right on again.

I'm jogging down the second-story walking track when a guy enters the weight room. I've never seen him before. His arrival catches my attention, so much so that I immediately slow to a brisk walk. He's not like the other gym members, whose faces I have memorized. He's not even wearing workout clothes. Instead, he's dressed in a button-down dress shirt and tie. Business casual. He's not carrying anything with him either—no water bottle, no sneakers, no duffel bag. His big eyes scan the room helplessly as he weaves his way through the sea of workout machines. He looks entirely lost, like he has never been to a gym before and doesn't know what he's supposed to do now that he's here.

I slow down more. I keep watching.

Eventually, the young man gives up, lacing his hands around his neck and craning his head toward the ceiling, eyes shut as if in desperate prayer. As he stands there, muttering something to himself, a staff member approaches him and offers him a bottle of Ambrosia. Visibly irritated, the man holds up his hands in refusal and walks away, shaking his head.

That's when he notices the walking track, and not long after that, me. We make eye contact for a split second before I avert my eyes, quickening my pace and drifting toward the outermost track. I'm too late, though. By now, he's bounding up the stairs and heading toward me. When he finally catches up to me, I jump, not having heard his footfalls over the loud music.

"Excuse me?" the man says in a rich but tentative baritone. "Could I ask you a question?"

Despite being surrounded by people, my social interactions at Mount Olympus have been brief and limited. The only people I really talk to are Sasha and Clarissa. I haven't wanted to talk to anyone since coming here. The idea of social interaction makes me sick. When the heart of Mount Olympus beats, *Go, go, go, go*, talking is a waste of time.

So the moment the stranger opens his mouth, I'm struck with a strange compulsion to grab him by the shoulders and shove him off the elevated walking track and into the weight room below.

Shit, when did I become so dark?

I realize I don't have to such violent extremes, though. Instead, I pick up the pace. I'm fresh off another dosage of Ambrosia and have plenty of energy to burn. I leave him in the dust, and as his pleas for me to slow down and listen grow steadily fainter, I smile. Before long, I lap him, and he's still trying to keep up. I catch a snippet of his ragged, asthmatic breathing and can't help but laugh.

And why am I laughing? I grit my teeth to stop the laughter. *I've gotten dark* and *mean, apparently.* A flicker of shame makes me slow my pace for a moment, but I brush it aside and throw myself into the run.

By the third lap, he appears to have given up on me entirely. He's clinging to the railing and waving to get the attention of other runners. They all ignore him, though, most of them speeding up to avoid him and a few flipping him off or shoving him roughly aside as they pass him.

When I pass him again, he kicks out his foot to trip me. It's too sudden for me to evade, and his foot snags on my ankle.

I'm airborne, my legs stumbling wildly. My heart dislodges itself in my chest as I fall for what seems like ages, then crash against the rough rubber flooring. I groan in agony, then jump to my feet, despite my pain, and roll to the outside of the track just in time to avoid a group of joggers who would have otherwise stampeded me without so much as an apology.

The asshole bites his lip as though to avoid smiling as he steps back and looks at his feet.

"What the hell is your problem?" I shout, stomping toward him. "You could have killed me!"

"I had to."

"Had to?" My voice sounds strangely shrill and frantic as I get up in his face, backing him up against the railing; his fearful eyes dart over the edge and back toward me. "No, what you have to do is stop harassing me while I'm trying to work—"

"I'm looking for someone," he says.

His answer takes me aback, though I hadn't really known what to expect from him in the first place. "So?" I cross my arms over my chest. "What does that have to do with me?"

"I saw you earlier," he continues. "And you seemed, I dunno—it seemed like you were...paying attention, I guess."

Sighing, I tap my foot to release the pent-up energy that I'm wasting by enduring this conversation. My hands twitch, and my skin feels clammy because I should be running, dammit. It's all I can do to keep from jumping back onto the track and leaving this guy in the dust, but there's this deep sorrow in his eyes. I can't bring myself to move.

Out of the corner of my eye, I see one of the ever-smiling gym staff members ascending the staircase, a clipboard tucked under his arm. He's glancing at us in a way that makes my stomach twist, though I'm not sure why.

"Walk," I command the stranger. I take a few steps forward, but he hesitates, so I grab one of his clean-pressed sleeves and tug him along. He glances in the direction of the staff member. "Don't make eye contact," I say through gritted teeth.

He must have obeyed because the staff member merely waves at us before scribbling something on his clipboard and disappearing into an office.

"Now," I say. "Talk. Who are you?"

"Gideon," he wheezes. "Gideon Wake."

I realize that he can't keep up with my pace, so I force myself to slow down. His expression relaxes in obvious relief.

"I'm Crystal," I say. "You said you were looking for someone."

He nods. "My brother, Elijah. He's tall—I'd say 6'4, at least. Black. Well, obviously. Bald. Has a tattoo of an eagle on his shoulder."

I roll my eyes. The idea of sifting through the faces of people I didn't care about irritates me to no end. "You realize there's over a thousand people here, right?"

Gideon reaches into his pocket and pulls out a wrinkled photograph. Handing it to me, he asks, "Does this help?"

I take the photo. As soon as I see the image of a man in an Air Force uniform, a sickly feeling explodes in my chest. Not only have I seen this guy—usually in the weight room, lifting torturous-looking barbells with no effort at all—he's one of the two people here I've talked to. My racing partner in the pool.

At least, for a while he was. The last three times I've been in the pool, I haven't seen him.

I nod. The picture quivers in my hand.

Gideon beams. "You know him!"

"Sort of." I can't look Gideon in the eye.

"That's great! Where was the last place you saw him? Is he still here?" My stomach turns. I open my mouth to answer, but an uncanny mixture of guilt and fear silences me.

"Well?" His eyes are wild, shifting from a look of impatience to grief to rage in the space of a few seconds. He takes a step forward as if he's ready to knock me back to the ground again.

"I—I don't know," I say. "I've seen him in the pool. That's where I saw him last. Last time I saw him, he was in the lane next to me. Then he got up and went to the locker room. Haven't seen him since."

"So he left today," Gideon says, eyebrows knitting together.

"No."

No one ever leaves. Do they?

"No?"

"I mean...maybe?" I hold up my hands, just as bewildered as him. "I don't know." Gideon's countenance darkens. The hope drops from his dark eyes, replaced by a look of intensity. Within seconds, he's in front of me, inches from my face and blocking my path.

"Are you screwing with me?" he asks.

"No, I swear. But—"

"But what?"

I grip the railing tightly, fingers curling tightly around the metal as I search for the right words. "You wouldn't understand."

"Try me." He extends his arms and takes a few paces backward. "I'm all ears."

The hair on the back of my neck stands up when I feel someone's eyes on me. Turning my head, I see two steely eyes peering through an office window. Staring me down.

"Keep walking!" I push past Gideon, grabbing him by the arm, and dragging him down the track with me.

We round the corner, and I lead Gideon to the staircase. As we descend, I say, "You've got to trust me when I say this. You promise? Promise not to think I'm crazy."

Gideon tenses up, his lips forming a thin line. "Just give me something. Anything."

Walking toward the weight room, I say, "Time is...weird here."

"Weird how?"

I take a deep breath. "I don't know when your brother disappeared. It could have been a day ago, a week ago, an hour ago. I don't know, though. The days kind of blend together."

A solemn look crosses Gideon's face as he processes my words. At last, he says, "That's impossible." And with that, he walks off, heading toward the pool and pushing past Clarissa and her tray of Ambrosia samples. I begin to salivate, and goosebumps rise all over my skin. I clench my fists, trying to fight the thirst.

"Wait!" I yell, taking off after him. "I can help!"

He ignores me, though, disappearing into the men's locker room without even a backward glance.

I give up. When the locker room door slams shut behind him, I'm suddenly overcome by an inexplicable feeling of sadness. I stand in the corridor, leaning against the cold concrete wall, my eyes sewn shut as I try to make sense of that long-forsaken emotion.

He's not going to find his brother. My head begins to ache as lost memories snap and hiss within my subconscious like snakes writhing toward the surface. He's going to lose everything. If he can't resist the Ambrosia, he'll be trapped here forever.

Like me.

What am I thinking? I shake my head, forcing a smile. *Trapped? I'm not really trapped.*

"Crystal!"

I open my eyes to see Clarissa standing before me with another damn cup in her hand. Doesn't she have anything better to do?

But on the other hand, I'm so happy to see her. The thirst hits me again, lighting a fire in the back of my throat, and I don't even try to resist it. Who am I kidding? And I hate myself for giving in again. Hate myself for being so weak, so enslaved by this addiction.

But... I'm not really enslaved. I reach for one of the cups with a tremulous hand. I'm not trapped.

I inhale the Ambrosia, and the clamor in my head goes quiet.

The suspicion and self-hatred diminishes, and that liquid strength bubbles up again. At Mount Olympus, bad feelings never last too long.

I'm not trapped. I'm happy.

I stare at the men's locker room, and I don't know why I'm standing here. Why am I not working out? Weird.

The gym is abuzz with activity. Sweat-slick bodies rush from room to room, from activity to activity. The music pounding from overhead bids me to join them, to *move, move, move, move...* But I'm stuck, and I'm not even sure why.

My mind is filled with a delicious emptiness, a cold vacancy. It's like my heavy soul has slipped out of my body, leaving it free to run, to jump, to do what it couldn't do before. But something is off. It's like in my soul's exodus, one remnant was left behind, a molding, festering piece keeping me from realizing my full potential. It's like when there's food left out somewhere in the house—you don't know where it is, but you know you'll go crazy if you don't get rid of it.

I feel the overwhelming urge to purge my spirit of whatever dark thought is scurrying around in my subconscious. But how?

After wandering around aimlessly, I notice a stream of people flooding into the room in the middle of the walking track: yoga class. My chest tightens as I remember faintly that I had a bad experience in that room. I stop short, my heart slamming against my chest. Just as I'm about to turn and run away, a familiar figure pokes his dreadlocked head through the open door. "You coming?" he asks.

My voice sounds small and quavery when I reply. "I don't know..."

Dreadlocks nods. "I know you had an intense session last time."

It's then that I remember falling into a vivid, painful memory during his meditation session—a memory that I've managed to bury since then. "Yeah."

Dreadlocks walks toward me, his bright, sympathetic eyes meeting mine. He places a hand on my shoulder. I should feel uncomfortable with a stranger getting so close to me, but instead, I feel comforted.

"I can sense some pain in your life," he says. "Deep-seated pain. If you try to ignore it, it will spread like roots and choke you from the inside out."

In my mind, I envision some dark shadow spreading roots, consuming everything in black. I shudder.

"If you want to rid yourself of this trauma once and for all..." He gestures to the open door to his studio. "There's no better place than here." Then, with a slight smile, he releases my shoulder and heads toward the studio. I stand there, pondering what Dreadlocks said. Part of me feels uneasy at the way he seemed to root through my thoughts and read them to me like pages from a diary. On the other hand, there's something reassuring about knowing that someone actually understands what I'm going through. Not only that, but that he can remedy it.

Before I have the chance to change my mind, I step into the studio, roll out a mat, and wait for instructions.

This ends now.

***

The session starts with simple yoga stretches. Despite my fading memories, my muscle memory remains intact; I follow the dreadlocked instructor step for step, move for move, and steadily, my racing heart settles down, and my churning mind slows to a crawl. Little by little, I let go of my anxiety, following the instructor's rich, soothing down into a state of relaxation I haven't felt in a while. Once again, I am aware of the pleasant emptiness in my mind, which is only magnified by my regulated breathing and slow, relaxing movements.

But when Dreadlocks asks us all to assume the lotus position and begin meditation, my heart skips a beat as I remember that this is the part where the ugly memories will come surging through. I'm tempted to get up and leave, but the instructor is looking right at me with those kind, stormy eyes of his, and I can't seem to move. Instead, I tentatively shut my eyes. Inhale deeply. And wait.

82

Chapter 11

As I follow Dreadlocks through the meditation exercise, my body goes limp and relaxed from head to toe. Mentally, I feel half awake and half asleep, my eyelids heavy. A distant voice in the back of my mind screams for me to wake up, that I don't want to go through with this. But that warning seems muffled, and I'm too deep into my trance to even attempt waking up.

"Now, reflect inward," the smooth voice says. "Your innermost desires...your ideal self. Picture that self in your mind."

And that's when the yoga studio fades away.

* * *

I'm sitting on the edge of a quiet pond, my feet dipped in the cool water. It's twilight, and the stars are just beginning to appear in the cornflower-blue sky. I stare across the pond and into the horizon, where water and sky seem to blend together. Taking in a deep breath, I stretch my limbs, relishing in the tranquility—after all the exercise I've done, it's nice to finally allow myself to rest.

Just when I'm starting to relax, though, my skin begins to prick when I'm aware of a presence before me: Looking up, I see me. No, not exactly. This woman has the same sand-colored skin, the same dark and curly hair, the same height. But that's not my body. Not by a long shot. The figure is perfectly sculpted, delicate and slender-framed overall, but somehow curved in all the right places. Her complexion is clear, and her porcelain smile seems to outshine the stars overhead. She's so beautiful that it makes my heart ache.

As if sensing my pain, the figure stops smiling at me. Gliding toward me through the water, she leans in and points at its surface without saying a word. I look down, obeying her silent instruction, and I see my true reflection in all its hideousness. I see the doughlike cheeks, the sea of pockmarks peppering my skin, and the wanton hair sticking out in every direction. Rage explodes in my chest at the grotesque sight. I slam my fist into the water, disrupting the reflection as tears threaten to spill over.

The beauty goddess straightens up, glaring at me. She shakes her head and opens her mouth to speak, but it's not my voice that comes out: It's that voice—the voice belonging to the one I thought I'd buried so well.

"Fat pig."

Then darkness.

* * *

Just when I think I'm going to emerge from the trance, I sink further down, past the abstract and into memory. My past has been pushed so far beneath layers of Ambrosia and exercise that I don't remember what's going to happen when I find myself on the toilet in Jace's and my old apartment building. But a sense of dread hangs over me as I clutch my knees, skin clammy, stomach cramping. I'm bleeding, and I can't seem to stop.

My head reels as anxious thoughts chase one another around in my brain. The terror is worse than the stabbing pain in my gut, for deep down, I know what is happening. But my mind refuses to form the words.

At last, the spasms end. The last of the blood slides into the toilet like some alien creature. Feeling dizzy, I rise, eyes closed. Tears leak out as I try to force myself to look at the carnage of my own body.

But I can't look at the damage for more than a few seconds. When I see the mass of blood clots and tissue, bile rises to my throat. I stumble to the bathtub and heave.

That was my baby!

That was my hope. The little universe forming within me. The precious thing that made my exile from my parents worth enduring. I wasted so many hours fantasizing about her—I always knew it'd be a girl. Holding her in my arms while she slept. Watching Jace teach her to ride a bike with no training wheels. Waving her goodbye as she climbed aboard a school bus for the first time. Show and tell. Science fairs. Senior prom. First dates. Wedding day.

These fruitless fantasies bombard me all at once, blurring together until all I see is red. Red like rage. Red like death.

I storm out of the bathroom and run headlong into Jace. He stands, stunned, waiting for me to explain my state of mind. Eventually, the words tumble out. "We...lost..." That's all I can manage before succumbing to a fit of sobbing. That's all he needs to hear.

At that moment, he is gentle as he lets me cry into his T-shirt. But I know, as if I'm watching the scene from outside my own body instead of reliving it, knowing all too well what comes next. I know how, later, he becomes bitter due to the loss. I know that his hope for the future died in that river of blood. I know that he learned to take his anger at the world out on me—and how I knew I deserved it.

Yes, my loathsome body deserved it. Every one of Jace's jabs at my physical imperfections, I internalized. Because it's not just about "ugliness." It's not just about fitting into Jace's expectations about what a woman should look like. No, for me, my physical ugliness is a reflection of something far more sinister.

My body is a killer. It killed our baby. It killed our hope. It killed Jace. And if Dr. Vance's warnings were as serious as they sounded, it would soon kill me.

I let go of Jace's shirt, run to our bedroom, and curl up in a ball on the floor. "I can't do this," I wheeze, tugging at my hair with both hands. I thought that I could be happy if I just refused to think about this dark moment in my life, but I now realize it was always there, lurking in the shadows, waiting for the right moment to come crawling back and claim me forever.

Just when I think I'll be stuck in the past forever, a deep, godlike voice echoes from overhead. *"Let the water wash it all away."*

Even though I'm inside, a raindrop strikes my cheek, then another. Within seconds, there's a torrential downpour in my cluttered bedroom. I hear Jace's voice calling me from outside the door, but he's muffled by the sound of rushing water.

"Wash it all away," I whisper. I stand, facing up into the impossible rainstorm. Shutting my eyes, I let the rhythm of the rain ease my racing thoughts. I'm becoming lighter with every passing second. The rain pounds against my eyelids, sinks into my skull, washing away the weight of my deep-rooted trauma. An urge, a familiar thirst, overpowers me: my body craves the holy water of this sudden storm like my lungs need air.

So I open my mouth and taste the sweetness of the rain. Only, it's not rain. I recognize this tangy sweetness.

Ambrosia.

When I open my eyes, I notice the water has risen to my waist. Not only that, but I'm no longer in my bedroom. The scene has faded, completely changed, replaced by a serene lake at dusk. No land to be seen for miles. Just blue reflecting blue and a scattering of stars twinkling above.

When the rain stops, I rack my mind, trying to remember how I arrived at this placid place. Knowing that I was somewhere else before—somewhere awful. I saw something terrible. But I can't remember what it was.

I sift through my memories for what seems like ages until a figure in the water catches my eye. A familiar face I've seen somewhere before. My reflection…but it seems wrong somehow.

Perfectly sculpted muscles. Flat stomach. Curved in all the right places. Clear complexion. Porcelain smile.

She's beautiful. She's me.

A new body.

I lean in to inspect the figure more closely until a baritone voice echoes over the water like a whisper of wind. I close my eyes and feel my soul floating out of the trance and into consciousness.

*　*　*

When I open my eyes—for real this time—I'm alone in the yoga studio, save for Dreadlocks, who's leaning against the wall, crossed-armed, and watching me emerge from the depths of my own mind. I scowl, trying to make sense of my surroundings, not even sure if they're real; everything else I saw felt real, after all. I put my hand to my face, and it comes away wet from tears. Why was I crying?

"You're awake." Dreadlocks steps toward me, then sits down, mirroring my cross-legged position. "Your visions seemed pretty…"

"Intense." I use his wording from earlier. But no matter how I try, I can't remember what I saw. The harder I try to remember, the faster the remnants of the experience slip away. It's like waking up from a dream that felt so real at the time, only to be left with a feeling.

And that's all I have: a feeling of being cleansed, purged of something painful. Cured. I smile.

Dreadlocks smiles back. "It's a good feeling, right? Getting rid of all that nastiness in your life?"

"Yeah." I don't bother wiping away the tear that slides down my cheek.

"I don't know what memories you just lost," he says. "But you sure as hell are better off without them."

"How do I make sure they stay gone?" The lingering shadow of whatever trauma I'd been freed from makes my chest tighten.

"You're safe as long as you're in Mount Olympus." With that, he stands and heads to the door. "I do hope you stay."

Alone in the studio, I ponder the yoga instructor's words. *You're safe as long as you're in Mount Olympus.* Why would I want to leave? Was I thinking about leaving before? I attempt to push through the fog in my mind, to think about life outside these walls. But I come up empty and only frustrate myself in the process.

When I try to think of the "intense vision" I experienced, all I can truly remember is the Ambrosia—its sweetness, its coolness, the way it washed away all the ugliness from my life. And suddenly, I'm thirsty.

And there it is again: the incessant heartbeat of Mount Olympus— *drink, move, drink, move.*

And after what I've been through, I'm all too happy to fall back in line.

So damn happy.

Chapter 12

After a shot of Ambrosia, I burn off my energy in the pool, thinking of nothing but how my limbs feel slicing through the cool water. I've become a machine, some alien being whose sole existence relies upon movement. I crave it until I finally run out of steam; then I crave the Ambrosia that sends me spiraling into my exercise addiction. But I'm happy, for once. Thanks to whatever happened in the yoga studio, I'm cured of the pain that held me back for so long. At last, I can carve my body into something beautiful. Something worth existing on this earth. Something I can be proud of when I look in the mirror.

When fatigue finally begins to settle in, I prop my arms up against the pool wall and look around idly. I'm about to reach for my bottle of Ambrosia when I catch sight of the door to the men's locker room. And my mind seizes up at the sight, giving me that eerie feeling like I've forgotten something important. I get an inkling—not so much an idea but the ghost of one—that I've stood outside that door, waiting for someone. But that doesn't make any sense. Why would I have been waiting for someone? The answer feels like it's on the tip of my tongue, but I push the thought away. I don't talk to people here, after all. I'm not here to make friends.

I give myself a mental shake and keep swimming.

Emerging from the pool at last, I see a guy I don't recognize—but I feel like I should. He walks swiftly, pacing past one of the windows to the corridor outside the aquatics room. There's something...almost familiar about him. He catches my stare, and I quickly avert my gaze.

As I step into the corridor and head toward the women's locker room, he follows after me, his dress shoes squeaking as he crosses the wet tile floor. *Dress shoes? Why is he wearing those?*

"Hey!" he says, finally catching up with me. He's panting and looks ragged. Sweat makes his dress shirt, which he's unbuttoned a bit, appear semi-translucent. He's ditched his stiff tie, and beads of sweat make his brow shine like polished stone.

I recognize him. I know I do. Details about his identity slowly fall into place like pieces of a jigsaw puzzle. My head hurts as I struggle to place a name to the face. *Garrett? Gerald? Gideon!*

"You were right, Crystal." He runs a hand through his black curls. His terrified eyes are magnified by his foggy glasses. He takes them off and wipes the fog away with his sleeve. "Something is wrong with the time here. I can't tell if I've been here a few minutes, a few hours—days?"

The last conversation I'd had with him clicks into my memory, tortuously slow. The pain in my head ratchets up as I drag up the buried details of the interaction.

I stare at him, dazed. Something about hearing him explain the strangeness of time here makes it all the more real. "Have you tried leaving?" I ask.

He looks down at his shoes. "I've thought about it. But I can't leave until I find my brother. The staff...they know something, and I just can't get anything out of them. If he's not still here, then they've done something to him."

"How did you know to come here anyway?" I pick up a thick white towel off a nearby bench and wrap it around my wet body. Even under the warmth from the oversized towel, I can't seem to stop shivering. "I hadn't heard of this place until..."

Until when?

Gideon leans against the tile wall and wipes the sweat from his face with his equally sweaty sleeve. "I had just left the police station when this guy approached me. Real athletic guy. One of those fitness buffs, you know? He asked me what was going on, and I told him my brother had gone missing. He told me to try this gym—that he thought he had seen him there a few times, and that maybe I would run into him."

"This 'fitness buff'... What did he look like?" I hold my breath as I await his answer.

Gideon launches into his description.

The blood drains from my face.

I knew it was Rory. Same hair color, same build, same gray eyes. *Gray eyes!*

I conjure up the faces of the staff, and I wonder how I could have been so blind. Rory, Sasha, Clarissa, Dreadlocks—they *all* have gray eyes. But how? They can't possibly all be related. But then, it would make sense if they were, right? I thought gray was supposed to be a rare eye color.

It's too strange to be a coincidence. But I hope it is.

I rub my temples, nursing another budding headache. It's like whenever I try to make sense of what's going on at Mount Olympus, my body resists it. But I can't seem to stop. A voice deep within my soul is begging me to piece together this puzzle, even as my body twitches for another cup of Ambrosia to kill that voice altogether.

Gideon notices my turmoil. "What's wrong? You've seen him?"

I snap out of my musing, giving Gideon a slight nod. "He told me to come here too."

"He must have gotten to Elijah," he says.

I open my mouth to protest. After all, I trust Rory. He's been nothing but good to me. More than good, in fact. But I can't seem to form the words to defend him because when I think about it, there is something *off* about my interactions with him.

Rather, it's weird that I can remember them with perfect clarity while the rest of my time at Mount Olympus is a blur. It took such effort to remember Gideon's name, much more so my life outside the walls of this gym. But I remember every interaction with Rory—every crooked smile, every compliment, every time he made my cheeks flush.

Gideon's arms are crossed over his chest as he looks into the distance, processing the information we exchanged. "This makes no sense," he says, putting his glasses back on as he crosses the corridor. He leans against the wall, towering over a water fountain and wiping sweat from his brow. "And damn, I am thirsty. I won't drink whatever these pushy staff are trying to offer me."

"It's just good that you've been able to resist the Ambrosia so long," I say weakly. "It...does something to you." I can't bring myself to say the words. Even as I'm trying to warn him, I feel my craving creep up within me.

He scoffs. "I knew I didn't trust those people." He stoops down and presses the bar on the water fountain, taking a long drink.

All of a sudden, I have an epiphany.

"You know," I say. "If we can find Ro—the guy who told us to come here—maybe we can get to the bottom of this. Maybe he'll know what happened to your brother."

Gideon has to have heard me. He's only a few feet away, after all. But he's still consuming gulp after greedy gulp of water, drinking faster with every passing second.

"I mean, he seems nice enough," I continue, speaking louder in case Gideon doesn't hear me over the stream of water. "All we'd have to do is ask. Right?"

Gideon's hands coil around the edge of the fountain. He leans in closer, practically inhaling the stream of water like it's air.

"You were thirsty, huh?"

No response.

My blood runs cold. I take a step closer, leaning down to examine his face. "Gideon?"

At length, he stops. He stands, eyes wild and unfocused, his pupils darkening his irises like twin eclipses.

And I know what's happened to him. I know it, but I can't accept it. I tell myself that he's just spaced out, or that maybe something in the distance has caught his attention. But as I look into his glassy eyes, I'm overcome with rage and panic when I realize the cruel trick Gideon had fallen for.

It's not a water fountain.

I grab him by his scrawny forearms and shake him once, hard. "Gideon!"

He roughly wrenches himself free of my grip, sending me crashing against the tile floor. There's an explosion of pain in the back of my head, and I see stars.

Even now, he's not looking at me.

"I have to go," he murmurs.

And just like that, he's gone, first strolling, then walking briskly, then breaking into an effortless sprint toward the workout room.

* * *

When Gideon leaves me alone in the corridor, I'm completely shaken. I watch him disappear for the second time, somehow knowing that he's taken my last chance at sanity with him. I sink onto one of the benches, putting my head in my trembling hands. Did I have someone like Gideon out there? A brother? A friend? Someone who would be looking for me?

More questions without answers. My entire body goes cold. There's a pressure in my head, a heaviness. I want nothing more than to curl up in my bed and cry myself to sleep.

How long has it even been since I've slept?

"Don't be stupid." I force myself to breathe. I don't need sleep any more than I need people. My nails dig into the bench, leaving little half-moons in the wood.

I have everything I need.

I look up and glare at the "water" fountain. My muscles lock up as I fight the urge to walk over there and follow Gideon's lead. I ball up my fists, turning my back on the fountain, but it's as though I feel its presence burning behind me, taunting me. I know exactly where this is going to lead, and I hate myself for turning around and giving in, but I have to.

Just one sip. One last time, I swear, then I'll leave.

When I lean into the cool stream of Ambrosia and gulp greedily, I do my best to hold onto the details of my conversation with Gideon. But when the lightning hits my bloodstream and my feet begin to itch for another adventure, all I can do is grit my teeth and try not to hate myself too much.

Drink, move, drink, move, goes my heartbeat. When does this cycle end?

Do I even want it to?

Chapter 13

From that moment on, I'm torn. Half of my mind makes a solid effort to bury my encounter with Gideon. I'm back in the rhythm of *drink, move, drink, move,* making the effort of remembering increasingly taxing. Part of me knows I need to remember him for some reason, and even as the details of our conversation fade, I still manage to hold onto his name. It's like Gideon is standing in an open grave, struggling for breath as dirt is poured all over him, trying to claw his way out.

But at last, the Ambrosia does its work, and once again, he's gone, six feet under, buried alive with so many other memories.

Rest in peace.

I'm on the stationary bike, riding up a digital mountainside, when the guilt returns, that guilt resulting from the ghosts of the memories I've killed, names and faces I've forgotten. Tears prick my eyes, mixing with the sweat dripping down my brow.

A thought bursts in my mind, not for the first time: *I hate myself!*

I sense another's presence nearby and crane my head around. Rory, a towel slung around his neck and looking perfect as ever in that compression shirt, his phone in his right hand. He lifts his phone to pause whatever he's been listening to, plucking one earbud out and sliding it into its case. "You all right, Crystal?" he asks, voice full of concern but gray eyes twinkling with affection.

Gray eyes... something important about gray eyes...

Memories thrash beneath six feet of dirt, gasping for air, begging to be heard.

Just then, I catch the familiar scent of cigarette smoke. Instinctively, I jerk my head toward the corner where I've seen...someone? That smell... Why is it important?

Why can't I remember?!

A tear leaks out of my eyes, and I turn my attention back to the digital mountainside. Rory places a hand on my shoulder.

"Hey," he says. "C'mon, you don't look so good. Take a break."

"I can't." The lightning from my last sip of Ambrosia still surges through my veins.

He stands in front of me, and even his perfect body isn't enough to distract me from my workout. The bike maximizes the resistance automatically, making me strain even harder as I stare at the small screen and not the beautiful man standing before me. But when Rory places a hand on mine, my resolve wavers. I glance up at him, another tear falling and mixing with my sweat as he runs soothing circles over my knuckles with his thumb.

"It's okay," he says. "You can take a break."

My legs gradually cease pumping the pedals. My lip quivers as I fight to keep breaking down entirely. And despite the way my heart is screaming *move, move, move*, I cave, letting him guide me off the bike and upstairs to the workout studio where he'd held the workout party session. Where I thought I purged the heaviness from my brain during that last meditation session.

Why do I remember all that and not... ? Tears continue to fall, and I quickly swipe them away. I hate that Rory has to see me like this, but he doesn't seem to mind, throwing a protective arm over my shoulder and pulling me close to his side, shielding me from the world.

* * *

There's nowhere to sit in the studio, other than on the yoga mats left out from an earlier class. Rory sits across from me, his legs almost close enough to touch and his steady gaze locked on mine.

In the silence of the studio, I let my emotions spill over. "I don't remember anything. I don't know what my life was like before..." I wipe away another tear as I try to remember the first time I walked through the doors of Mount Olympus. "I know I did it to myself, somehow. Like, this is what I wanted. But still, I feel like I'm going crazy."

Rory places a hand on my knee, stroking the skin gently. He waits.

"And I can't stop," I say.

"What do you mean? Can't stop what?"

"Can't stop..." I gesture to the workout studio. "All of this. Can't stop drinking the Ambrosia, which makes me want to work out, which makes me want to drink more, which makes me want to work out, which makes me want to—"

Rory scoots closer and puts a hand on each shoulder. "Hey, it's okay," he croons. "Take a deep breath."

I inhale deeply and exhale through my nose. "You know what I'm talking about, right? Tell me I'm not insane."

He shakes his head. "Of course not. Ambrosia can be a little...intense. It affects everyone differently."

Intense... Wasn't that Dreadlocks's word?

"I want to get out of here."

Rory knits his eyebrows together, clearly bewildered. "'Get out of here'? What do you mean?"

I open my mouth to explain, but his confused expression makes the words die on my tongue.

"If you want to leave, just leave." Rory laughs as if I'd said something funny. "I mean, this isn't prison."

"I will," I say, but my eyes drop to the floor.

There's a pause. "You do *want* to leave, right?"

I sigh. "Rory, tell me something. Your memory...you're not having the same problem, right? Like, you can remember everything clearly."

He shifts uncomfortably, averting his eyes from mine for a split second. "Of course."

"Then..." I bite my lip, half-afraid to ask the question. "Did I ever tell you anything about myself before I lost my memories? Did I ever tell you about my life? My family?"

He looks down, frowning. This is answer enough for me.

"I just want to know if it's worth it," I tell him. "I don't know. It's just that maybe..."

He finishes my sentence. "Some memories are worth burying?"

We're silent for a long moment, the weight of our conversation hanging over us. Finally, Rory stands and extends a hand to help me up.

"You only told me a little about your past," Rory says. "But there's a way I can help fill in the gaps. Then you can decide for yourself what you want."

I let him help me up, and his hand lingers in mine long enough to make my heart stutter. "What do you mean?"

"It's a little hard to explain," he says. "It's better if I just show you."

* * *

Rory leads me out of the workout area and back to the lobby, a room I haven't set foot in ages. Sasha's desk is vacant, which strikes me as odd. Rory doesn't seem fazed, though. He gives the room a cursory glance, then reaches down to unlock the half-door that separates Sasha's circular desk from the rest of the lobby. He stands on the other side and offers me his hand.

"You sure she won't mind us being in her space?"

"Nah. Sasha and I are close." Then suddenly, his eyes brighten, and he plants himself in Sasha's desk chair and crosses his legs. "Welcome to

Mount Olympus, darlin'!" he says, mimicking Sasha's chipper Southern belle timbre.

I crack up, applauding his performance. "Well done." I follow Rory's lead, stepping through the half-door onto the other side. "It's like she's still here."

Beaming with boyish charm, he stands, then walks to the wall opposite the desk, stopping in front of a door. It seems vaguely familiar, though I don't remember why.

"Ready?" The childlike expression on his face has been replaced by one of solemn reverence.

I nod, though I'm not sure what I'm supposed to be ready for. He opens the door, and I follow him in.

The room is dark, save for the ghostly light coming from a wall of security televisions. My eyes can't focus on more than one TV at a time, and they jump from screen to screen.

"A security room?" I say. "I don't understand how this will help me."

Rory grins. "It's not just a security room."

I raise an eyebrow at him, glancing around the room. After a good, long look, I say, "Nope, I'm pretty sure it's just a security room." My gaze falls on a box labeled "Lost and Found." Peering into the empty box, I think, *I lost something here...Something important.* The thought makes me shiver unexpectedly, so I brush it aside, returning my attention to Rory.

Rory chuckles, the TV screens illuminating his already bright eyes. "Here's the thing," he says. "It seems to me that you suspect that there's more to Mount Olympus than meets the eye. Well...you're right."

My heart beats a little faster.

"See, Mount Olympus is just a piece of a much larger operation," Rory explains. "A technological superpower, if you will, with a lot of experimental projects." He gestures to the flickering screens. "This is one of them."

I look back at the screens, watching the gym members, distant and small like ants in God's eye. I can't help but feel that Rory's pranking me.

He points to a small rectangular panel beneath the screens, connected to the wall. "Touch it," he instructs. "Then take a look at the screens."

My eyebrow is still raised as I look from Rory to the panel, to the screens.

"Trust me," he says. "It sounds crazy, but...this will show you what you're looking for."

I take a deep breath and prepare myself. Yes, what Rory's suggesting does sound crazy. But after all I've been through lately, who am I to judge? Taking a deep breath, I tentatively touch the panel. Within seconds, it pulsates with cold blue light, illuminating my hand and making every hair on my body stand up. Looking up, I see the images on the screen fade to black one at a time. The panel beneath my hand fades like a dying star, and then the whole room is bathed in blackness.

"Great. I broke it."

"Just wait." I can hear the smile in Rory's voice.

No sooner than the words leave his lips does a screen in the upper left-hand corner flicker back to life, followed by one in the center of the wall. One by one, each screen reboots itself, and blurry images reveal themselves in the ghostly light.

"It's working," Rory says. But he's not smiling anymore. He's looking at the screen dead in the center of the wall.

I open my mouth to ask what he sees, but when I look, the image knocks the wind right out of me. It's a young man with short-cropped hair and an ever-present sneer. He's half-dressed and screaming at a young, half-crazed woman: me.

"Jace!" The name bursts through six feet of dirt, gasping for air.

"Boyfriend?" Rory asks.

"Ex."

Watching us argue from this bird's-eye view makes my cheeks warm with shame. I cringe, listening to the angry words fly from my lips, and my stomach twists up in knots when I remember...

"Fat pig." The words are distant, half-garbled, but they sting all the same.

The door slams, and he disappears from my life forever.

Tears stream down my face when I remember...remember what comes next.

"What a douchebag," Rory mutters.

And although he is right, there's something about Rory saying it that makes me feel defensive. I turn my back to the screens.

"What? It's true!" Rory says. "I mean, you can't still have feelings for this guy, can—"

"I killed him."

The words stop Rory in his tracks. "I'm sorry, what?" I turn to face him.

"You heard me. I killed him."

Rory's eyes widen, and he scans the screen, looking at assorted images from my life. Some memories are crucial, but most are mundane. "Yeah, I'm not seeing that here," he says at last.

I cross my arms over my chest, trembling with the effort of trying not to cry again. "You don't understand! He died because of me. Just like my..." Another memory thrashes beneath fathoms of water, but I force it down.

Rory turns back to face me, waiting intently.

"After that fight, he got in a car accident." I blink hard, but I can't stop the tears from flowing. "We wouldn't have fought if he hadn't cheated on me. He wouldn't have cheated if I weren't a hideous, fat pig!" I collapse in a desk chair in front of the security cameras, putting my head in my hands. "It's my fault."

The silence that follows is deafening. Rory sits down next to me, rubbing my back as I lose the will to fight back the tears. I ugly cry, wishing that the sound of my weeping were loud enough to drown out the cacophony of voices from the past I only just now learned to forget.

"That's a heavy burden to bear," Rory says at last.

And I feel so relieved that he didn't say, "It's not your fault," or, "He deserved it," or the other bullshit I've heard throughout the years.

I don't want sympathy or comfort. Never have. Never will.

I want to feel the knife of guilt twisting in my heart. I want to feel punished.

More than that, I want to forget.

"I don't blame you for wanting to bury all that," Rory whispers. "It's okay."

I lift up my head and wipe away my tears. I asked him if it was worth it, leaving Mount Olympus and figuring out what memories I've lost.

I think I have my answer.

There are other screens, of course. I don't want to look at them. Quick glances bring pangs of shame, guilt, hurt, anger. Turning away, I stand, eyes lost in the darkness of the room.

Rory breaks the solemn silence with a sigh, then takes a couple steps away from me. His back turned toward me, he approaches the flickering screens, halting in front of them and nervously tapping his foot.

"What's wrong?" I ask.

"Nothing. I just…" Rory inhales deeply, ceasing the tapping. "I was thinking about showing you something, but…"

I consider saying something encouraging, but his stance and body language show the struggle with whatever decision he's facing. I stay silent, but inwardly, I'm willing him, *Please, please show me something. I want to know you better.*

As if he's heard my pleading, he resumes his slow walk toward the security screens. He places his palm on the panel, and just like that, the miserable scenes from my own life fade to black, leaving the whole room in darkness. Then, just like before, one screen, followed by another and another, begins to glow with static snow. Once all the screens are lit, that's when the clips begin.

"I lied to you earlier," Rory says, his voice flat. "I've buried some memories too."

My heart sinks as my eyes wander from screen to screen. Despite everything I assumed about my seemingly perfect crush, his life doesn't appear to be much better than my own.

There's a screen that shows child Rory clutching a teddy bear while his parents scream at each other in another room.

Another shows him sitting alone in a school cafeteria, his stomach growling as he stares vacantly at his empty lunch table.

In another one, a scrawny, bespectacled Rory sits on a school bus, burying his head in a thick novel, trying his damnedest to ignore the bullies who taunt him from the seat behind him. He clutches the book to the point where his hands shake, but he can't bring himself to confront his tormentors.

"There it is." Rory's voice seems distant and small, not at all like the confident and charming one I had grown so fond of. When I turn, I see Rory pointing at the screen in dead center. "This..." He puts his hands together as if in prayer, covering his mouth, seeming to grow smaller as he watches the scene.

This scene depicts teen Rory, still scrawny and bespectacled, being admonished by his father, a hulking, intimidating figure. At first, this clip mirrors that of the bullies on the bus—his father paces before him, spitting obscenities as he holds a crumpled report card in his hand. Young Rory scowls, his fingers digging into the arm of the couch where he sits, tapping one foot.

Suddenly, Rory's father ceases his pacing and plants himself in front of his son. Infuriated by Rory's lack of response, he grabs him by the hair, forcing the boy to stand. Rory winces in pain, eyes squeezed shut.

I steal a glance at present-day Rory. He's wincing too, and his foot won't stop bouncing as he watches the scene play out.

On the screen, Rory's father holds his son by the hair for what seems like hours, still screaming and demanding a response. Young Rory cringes and tries to free himself, but refuses to cry. After a torturous moment, Rory's father releases him, and Rory stumbles backward, forcing himself to stand on wobbly legs.

Rory's father sneers. "You're a fucking failure."

And the look in teen Rory's eyes is the look of someone who's come unhinged.

What follows is an all-out brawl. Rory throws the first punch, making his father stumble back several feet from sheer surprise alone. The man's shock quickly gives way to rage, and he charges Rory, knocking him to the ground. I back away from the screen, my eyes watering until all I see are blurry shapes writhing and twitching on the screen.

At last, the brawl ends, and teen Rory emerges the victor. His glasses are broken, his face bruised, and his nose leaking blood. But he stands.

His father does not. Instead, he rolls over, propping himself up against the wall. The man's eyes are swollen shut as he points a shaking finger in Rory's direction. "You get the hell out of my house, boy! You come back, and I call the cops!"

Young Rory just stands there, as if not understanding.

"Get out!" Rory's father tries to stand but falls backward. "I don't ever want to see you again."

The scene fades to static snow.

My mouth drops open. I know I should say something, but I can't seem to form the right words.

Thankfully, Rory speaks first. "I just figured you should know." He turns to face me, but his eyes are set on some space between his feet. "You're not the only one who feels...cast out. Guilty. I get it."

I nod. "I'm so sorry."

He shrugs, his lips curving upward in a smile that doesn't reach his eyes. "What's past is past. Best I can do is forget about it and move on."

Forget about it and move on. Isn't that all I've ever wanted? Isn't that what Mount Olympus has given me?

Even under the influence of Ambrosia, it's been hard for me to truly surrender, to let go of the small hope that there's something out there that might make life on the outside worth living. But these security screens confirm what I've thought all along: there's nothing for me out there. Only pain. Heartbreak. Ugliness. Regret.

Forget about it.

"What are you thinking?" Rory asks, his eyes shining with unshed tears.

"I think...I think I'll stay here a little longer."

He wraps an arm around my shoulder and pulls me close to his side. He smells like salt and cedar. I wrap my arms around his waist, inhaling deeply, and his fingers thread through my curls, gently rubbing my scalp in a way that only makes me lean into him more.

"I'll be here if you need me," he murmurs in my ear.

As I close my eyes, the lights from the security screens continue to flicker, their pulsating light making my head pound. So I bury my head into Rory's chest until my vision is nothing but comfortable darkness.

Chapter 14

The trip to the security room is just the push I need to get me back on track. When I'm overwhelmed with worries like writhing corpses beneath earth and water, I push them back down. Push them far, far down where I can't hear them scream.

No, I decide. I won't listen. *I have better things to do.*

By now, I've noticed a significant change in my physical appearance. While I'm no supermodel, my sweatpants don't fit as well around my waist as they used to. I have to tighten the drawstring that holds them up. Gone is the baby face that I've always loathed. For once in my life, I'm making progress.

The only time I'm able to slow down is whenever I pass one of Mount Olympus's many mirrors. No matter what I'm doing, I have to admire my own reflection for just a little while.

Everything is fine. I'm unburdened by bad memories, I'm sculpting my ugly body into something more desirable, and I've transcended most human needs thanks to the Ambrosia.

Yes, for once in my life, everything is fine.

But then I see a man below who works out in dress pants and a sleeveless undershirt. *Who dresses like that to work out?* The sight of him fills me with a strange sense of guilt and dread. Suddenly, all I want is to shatter the walls of this utopia and run straight home—if I even have no home to go to. No matter how much I run, or how hard I swim, or how hard I push myself, whenever I see that man with the bad clothes and the sad eyes, I'm haunted by my hollow mind. The emptiness that once comforted me is now terrifying.

Even more unsettling are some of the behaviors I'm noticing from other gym members.

Drink. I'm inhaling Ambrosia greedily from the fountain outside the pool. When I stop, I look through the window and see a young woman in a swimsuit sitting on a bench, holding a diamond ring in her trembling hands. Tears stream down her weathered face, and she mutters something to herself.

As I draw closer to her, I read her lips: "Why can't I remember you?"

The fiery-haired lifeguard notices the woman's odd behavior. Descending from his tower, he tucks his rescue tube in one hand and a yellow-labeled bottle in another. He approaches the woman, extending the bottle. She hesitates but tearfully accepts. And then she's smiling as if she hadn't just had a mental down a second ago.

I stare at the woman through the Plexiglas. Her smile doesn't touch her eyes, those blue orbs reflecting the emptiness that I feel inside. And that realization doesn't even surprise me, not an epiphany so much as a cold fact—one I already knew perhaps on a subconscious level.

I am empty.

The longer I watch this now-smiling woman bobbing up and down in the water, the more pissed off I get.

Is that what I look like?

A blurry memory of my own encounter with that same lifeguard resurfaces. I'd been distressed. I'd wanted to leave. But all he had to do was shove a bottle in my face, and all that worry simply vanished. There has to be something wrong about that.

A ghostly flicker of memory—cruel words, a slammed door, death—flashes in my mind again. I tear myself away from the window and make myself forget.

I have better things to do.

Move. I'm on the stationary bike when I see a young man who can't be any older than eighteen staring at the window for what must be a solid half-hour. He clenches and unclenches his fists. His ashen body shakes in irregular spasms. I hear him rattling off numbers, counting the passing seconds as if to distract himself from whatever torment is swirling within his own body. He suddenly stiffens. I watch as he runs to the other end of the room and vomits a stream of neon-yellow fluid into a trash bin. He lies on the floor for several moments before an attractive lady in a yellow polo kneels over him, a bottle of Ambrosia in her hand. She stays there, silent for a long, painful moment as the boy turns away and curls up on the floor in a fetal position. His whole body shakes.

There isn't an ounce of sympathy on the staff woman's face.

A part of me wants to run over there and shove the woman away. To scream at her to leave him the hell alone. But part of me knows she's got the quick fix that will put an end to the boy's misery. I try not to look, but I can't seem to tear my eyes away from the scene.

My heart pounds frantically as a look of defeat falls over the young man's face, making his limbs fall slack. Rearing up like a pissed-off snake, he snatches the bottle from her hands. He sobs uncontrollably and beats the floor with his free fist as he downs one bottle, then another, and another.

His sobbing gives way to hysterical laughter.

I blink away the stinging in my eyes, wishing the bike wasn't stationary and could take me far, far away from here. And yet, the irony of the situation isn't lost on me—I'm moving fast and getting nowhere.

But when I see Rory on the other end of the room, giving me a thumbs up and flashing a warm smile, I close my eyes. Breathe deeply. Push the feeling of helplessness down, down, down.

Forget.

Drink. I've run out of steam on the walking track and am about to visit Clarissa and her free sample tray. As I'm slowing to a walk, an elderly man jogs in front of me and then, to my horror, climbs up the protective railing. He clings to a metal bar that connects the railing to the ceiling, but his body sways slightly, unable to keep balance on the slight metal railing.

I halt dead in my tracks, stunned, unable to process what I'm seeing. For the longest time, he just stands there, clinging to the pole for dear life but staring down, as if steeling himself for the dizzying drop. Slowly, one hand releases the metal bar.

My heart drops out of my chest. *He's gonna jump!*

And the worst part is, no one is stopping him. Myself included. I'm paralyzed with horror at what I'm seeing, so much so that I can't even make myself turn away.

The old man looks down from the dizzying height, gritting his teeth as gravity makes him sway between life and a painful plunge to death. My mind screams at me to run, to scream, to do something! But it's as if the floor has turned to quicksand beneath my feet, holding me captive yet making me sink slowly down.

Three staff members appear out of nowhere and are at the old man's side within seconds, wrapping their arms around his unsteady legs and guiding his body gently to the floor. He hurls curses at his saviors but doesn't actively fight the young men until he's touched the ground. A couple of them pin his arms and legs down while another holds a bottle of Ambrosia directly in front of his face.

"Please," the man wheezes through his tears. "Take that stuff away from me."

The staff members don't reply.

I'm frozen in place as I listen to the man weeping and begging for the Ambrosia to be taken away. It's like I'm listening to someone being tortured.

When the man doesn't cease his pleading, the staff member holding the Ambrosia bottle opens it up and pours it into the man's mouth. He sputters and coughs, trying to rid himself of the stuff, but it's clear that the drink has done its work. After a few seconds, the old man's body relaxes. He shuts his eyes. When the anguished look fades from his countenance, the yellow-clad staff members release their grip on him and step away. He smiles, turns on one heel, and breaks into a sprint. A few tears slide down his weathered face.

Not long after that, I'm curled up on the floor of a locker room shower, wishing that the stream of warm "water" could wash away the incident on the walking track from my memory.

I don't even want Ambrosia anymore, I realize. The thrill it used to give me is gone. The ecstasy is gone. But I need it to function. It comes as naturally as filling a car with gasoline.

Move. As I approach the mirror near the walking track, I slow to a stop once again to admire myself. But now, the pride I've felt before is quickly replaced with disgust.

I'm still losing weight. That much is apparent. But there's something off about the image blinking back at me. Something less than human. Something odd about the way the muscles in my calves and biceps bulge. It's as though my body has been pinched and molded in all the wrong directions, like clay in the hands of an incompetent sculptor. I'm disproportional. Deformed.

I step closer to the glass, transfixed. A sudden memory explodes in my mind—me, twenty pounds ago, staring at myself in the mirror and willing myself to go to Clarke's Gym. The depression and self-hatred that washed over me like a tidal wave. Back then, I would have killed for the body I have now, despite its strangeness. Back then, my reflection filled me with such disdain and disgust. Now, I have the body I wanted, but what good is it?

I'm a body without a soul. A pretty vessel containing nothing.

But closing my eyes, I take myself back, back to the room with the wall of unhappy memories. Memories I've just now learned to rid myself of once again.

"Crystal." Rory's voice makes me jump. Turning around, I see him standing next to me, that disarming smile of his still lighting up his face. "You okay?"

His smile reels me back in. "Yeah. I'm good," I tell him.

But when I see a flash of platinum blonde hair sail past me, I jump. A model-thin, bright-haired woman is jogging down the hall, completely oblivious to everyone around her.

I know her.

"Hey, you okay?" Rory's voice seems far away.

The young woman is long gone, but I can't stop staring in the direction she's headed toward. She's so deeply buried in my foggy subconscious that I can't remember her name. Seeing her is like seeing a ghost, though. I'm suddenly cold. Suddenly uncomfortable.

Rory waves his hand over my face, and I blink. "Where'd you go?" He steps in front of me, holding a bottle of Ambrosia in his hand. My mouth waters, but I try to look past him. "You okay?"

I grit my teeth, trying to resist, but my eyes keep going to the bottle of precious liquid. He notices and practically shoves the drink in my hand. After only a moment's hesitation, I wrench off the cap and down empty the bottle's contents.

He smiles at me, but I can't help but think there's something sinister behind those steel-bright eyes. The moment of unease passes, and I surrender to that familiar, delicious surge of adrenaline.

"Better?" The malice is gone from his face.

"Yeah," I say. "Everything is fine."

* * *

I lie on my back in the therapy pool, eyes closed, floating alone, relishing in my own numbness.

I am empty.

The water is still. All is silent, save for the incoherent music muffled by the water that covers my ears.

I am empty, and I don't care.

Empty of fear, of sadness, of desire, of the writhing tangle of emotions that once defined me.

Vaguely, I recall being someone else—someone weaker, both physically and emotionally.

But thinking of that person is like trying to recall a past life.

I open my eyes and stare at the fluorescent lights overhead. I lazily move my limbs through the water, dragging my body toward the pool ladder.

I am empty. But it doesn't scare me. Maybe it used to, but not anymore.

I've been transformed. Inhuman.

Superhuman.

My head knocks against the pool wall, but I feel no pain. The thirst returns with a wicked vengeance, and I climb out, ready to obey it.

Ready to surrender.

Chapter 15

He's far below me, busting his butt on a treadmill. I try to keep from looking at him as I run the elevated track, but my eyes can't help drifting toward him all the same.

It's harder to recognize him at first because he's wearing real workout clothes now: a yellow Mount Olympus T-shirt and a pair of black sweatpants, probably provided by the staff.

As much as I don't want to admit it, there's no denying the fact: I know him. He's significant in my life somehow.

Don't look, don't look, don't look... I shut my eyes as I pass him, and I try to ignore the pang in my chest that comes from merely knowing he's there. *Don't remember.*

When I pass him the next time, I can't tear my eyes away, though. I watch him running like hell on the workout machine, fists clenched. Are those tears or sweat?

The questions pile up. I don't know his name. I don't remember why he's important, and I don't understand the feeling of sadness that overcomes me whenever I look at him.

I don't know why he has a photograph on the panel of his treadmill. My mind screams that I don't want to know, screams for me to push down the questions clawing their way to the surface of my consciousness.

I can't help it, though. Curiosity compels me to descend the staircase and head toward him. I cut through the horde of sweating bodies and approach his treadmill. Standing a few feet away, I look at the picture on the panel of his machine.

It's a photograph of a young man in an Air Force uniform.

My heart skips a beat as a memory struggles to the surface of my addled mind. *That guy in the photo... I know him too!*

But I don't *really* know him.

He's lost. Buried.

The man on the treadmill looks at me sideways, agitated. I take a step back, but I can't tear my eyes away from the photo on the machine, even as my head begins to ache with the strain of dragging memories from the earth.

And then, after a long, agonizing moment, I remember him.

I remember everything.

His name is Gideon, and his brother's name is Elijah. He came to Mount Olympus to find his missing brother, and he was sucked into this trap just like I was.

He has a life outside these walls. And so do I.

And I know I don't have long before this moment of clarity passes. "Gideon!" I shout at him as he stares at the wall, and his legs pump furiously.

"Gideon, snap out of it!"

No response.

I shake his arm. I slap it, hard. He glares hard at me and then returns his gaze to the wall.

"Gideon, we have to find your brother!"

The hairs on the back of my neck stand up as I feel eyes on me. Glancing back, I see a man and a woman dressed in yellow and gesturing toward me. The man picks up a two-liter bottle of Ambrosia. They head toward me.

But I remember something else about Gideon and the first time he caught my attention.

I stick out my foot and make him stumble on the treadmill.

There's something almost comical about the way Gideon's legs flail about cartoonishly before he falls flat on his stomach. The treadmill makes him zip onto the floor, and he rolls over on his back, staring at me, stunned.

And then furious.

The staff members are now jogging in my direction.

"Gideon!" I say, leaning over him. "It's Crystal. You have to remember me. We have to find your brother! We have to get—"

He rears up and clenches his fist as if to strike me, but I dodge it just in time, feeling the air whiz past my cheek.

The yellow shirts are nearly upon me.

So I take off, making my way toward the locker rooms connected to the swimming pool. Gideon follows, spitting curses as he chases me. I can't hear the two yellow-clad staff members, but I know they aren't far behind and that they will continue in their pursuit, even if Gideon miraculously remembers who I am and why I did what I did.

It's useless to run from them, but it's all I can do.

I tear down the corridor, heading toward the women's locker room. Fighting to keep my balance, I tread the slippery floor, pushing past women in swimsuits and towels. Hoping, praying, that Gideon won't follow me there. He only hesitates outside the door for a few seconds, too pissed to be held back by any scruples about entering the women's locker room.

Shit.

I run harder than I have since my coming here, my last dose of Ambrosia giving me strength but my fear making my steps clumsy. Then an idea comes to me, one that will at least keep Gideon off my tail.

In the corridor that connects the men's and women's locker rooms with the aquatics center, there are several single-stalled unisex changing rooms, complete with bathrooms and showers. As Gideon continues gaining on me, I find an empty changing room and head for it. My foot slips in a small puddle of water and I fall, slamming my nose against the sink. I hear a crack. Blood gushes.

Looking up, I see Gideon—wild-eyed and feral—roaring at me as he continues in his rage-induced chase. He's mere feet away from me when I slam the door in his face and lock it. I crawl to the other end of the small room, trembling as his fists pound against the door, making the room shake.

"Gideon, listen!" I say, my voice sounding nasally as I pinch my nose to stop the flow of blood. "You have to find your brother. You have to find a way out of here!"

He throws his entire body against the door, and the impact is so hard that I fear the steel door will fly off its hinges. I curl into a tighter ball, then try again.

"Stop drinking the Ambrosia, Gideon," I plead, tears falling freely and mixing with the blood. "It's making you—"

There's a sudden sound like a rip of electricity, and all at once, Gideon's banging ceases. I hear fabric sliding against steel, then a heavy thump against the ground.

"Gideon?"

Silence. Then a sound like a heavy sack being dragged across the floor, then nothing.

"Gideon!"

Nothing.

Three gentle knocks resound on the door. A soft, polite sound that makes my flesh crawl.

"Hello?" a honeyed male voice croons. "Crystal? You okay in there?"

I feel the blood drain from my face at the sound of my name being spoken by the unfamiliar voice. Shaking all over, I brace myself for my inevitable demise. Of course, Gideon could not make it through the locked door, but surely the staff would have a key.

"Sounds like you took a pretty bad fall," a female voice says, heavy with concern. "We should take a look to make sure you're all right."

I open my mouth to speak, but the words die on my tongue. Tremors rock my body, making my teeth knock together.

"That psycho's been dealt with," the male says. "You don't have to be afraid of him."

That snaps me out of my paralysis. I crawl toward the door and shout, "What did you do with him? What did you do with his brother?"

A mocking laugh. "What do you mean—?"

"Enough!" I snap, sending my free fist crashing against the steel door. "I know what you're doing. I know you've been drugging us. I know you don't want us to leave. I know you're making us forget…" And there it is again, that grief that comes from missing something and not even knowing what.

Blood-curdling silence. The male voice says, "So, you're a smart girl."

"That's too bad," says the female voice.

Dread hits me like a freight train with the realization that I am right.

That they aren't even denying my accusations.

"W-what happens now?" I stammer, not feeling as bold as I had a few seconds ago.

A pause. I imagine the staff members looking at each other with those sickening smiles as they plot how they will end me. At last, the female says, "You're in control of that, sweetie. You can come out of that bathroom, drink your Ambrosia, and go on like this never happened. Do as you're told." She lets out an exasperated sigh. "For *once*, you could stop trying to fight us."

"Or," the male says, his tone laced with wicked glee. "You can stay in there and starve. Quit cold turkey, so to speak. You won't enjoy that, though. I can promise you that."

"Probably won't survive it," the female says, matter-of-fact.

With some effort, I drag up a memory about the young man I'd seen in the weight room, throwing up into the trash can before finally giving into his addiction. I remember how he shivered, how he grew ashen, how he looked like he was in unfathomable pain.

Cold turkey.

Door Number One means I'll stay relatively comfortable and happy—at least, for a while. But I think about the way I and the other gym members have been living—trapped, enslaved, mindless—what kind of existence is that?

Then there's Door Number Two. Suppose I manage to get...clean. What then? Will the staff just let me go? No, I'll have to escape, but how can I do that when I'm weak from withdrawals?

"Well?" I hear the sound of fingernails drumming against the bathroom door.

Am I going to die here?

If I'm going to die, I want to remember the life I had before first. I want to be a person for just a little while longer instead of a body on a treadmill.

"I'm staying..." I say. And as the words leave my mouth, I almost wish I could take them back.

A stretch of tense silence passes. I wonder if their faces show disappointment or sadistic pleasure.

My bet is on the latter.

"Suit yourself," the female says.

"We'll be back," her companion says. "In case you change your mind." Their synchronized footsteps against the tiles signal their retreat.

I release a sigh of relief and slide down the door onto the floor. Waiting for the adrenaline to die down, I try to control my ragged breathing. Truly alone for the first time in God knows how long, I ponder my spontaneous moment of defiance.

What the hell was I thinking? The idea of going a few moments, much less a lifetime, without Ambrosia makes me feel queasy. But I breathe deeply, trying to calm my thoughts.

"I need this," I tell myself. "I can't stay here forever."

But there's another voice I've got to combat all the while. One that incessantly asks, *Why can't I?*

I know one thing: without Ambrosia, my memories are going to return. Hopefully, they'll give me the drive that I need to endure whatever hell I've subjected myself to.

Chapter 16

Stuffing my still-bleeding nose with tissue, I stretch my limbs and pace the room. My room. It may be a bathroom, but it's all mine. I realize now that it's been a while since I've had any privacy. I hadn't really wanted it before.

A sense of pride makes my heart glow. I congratulate myself for making this difficult choice, and I think about how clean I'll feel with the toxic Ambrosia finally flushed from my body.

Speaking of clean, I'm just now noticing how badly I smell. With no one else around to confuse my sense of smell, the pungent odor radiating from my pits takes my breath away. I decide to take a shower, but when I turn the handle, no water comes out.

Great. Guess I'll have to deal with it. I slide to the bottom of the shower and hold my knees to my chest, tilting my head down and pinching my nose. When it finally stops bleeding, I keep the tissue in a little longer to block out some of the smell.

The room is silent, save for the muffled murmur of music coming from outside the door. It's a comforting sound, one that settles my nerves and fills my head with drowsiness.

Yawning, I lie on the shower floor. I know I need to sleep if I want to prepare my body for life without Ambrosia. But my mind can't seem to shut up. Eventually, my eyelids grow heavy, and I fall into a fitful sleep. The first sleep I've had in what seems like an eternity.

* * *

When I awaken from my nap, the effects of my last Ambrosia dosage have worn off—I'm not feeling anywhere near as strong as earlier. My fingers twitch, so used to reaching for a bottle or a cup to abate this feeling of weakness. In time, the cold, damp room feels several degrees colder than it did when I first entered it. My teeth chatter and my knees knock together. My skin is feverishly hot, but cold sweat coats my brow.

Soon, I'm nauseous. There's a nasty taste in the back of my mouth that makes my saliva hard to swallow. My stomach swirls, and I scramble over to the toilet. Leaning over, I vomit up a stream of bright yellow liquid. Just when I think it's over, I'm clinging to the toilet again.

I can't help but think about how just one sip of Ambrosia would be enough to settle my queasiness along with all the other unpleasant symptoms I'm enduring. The thought makes my hands shaky, and I quickly shut it down, willing my hands to steady as I clench them into fists.

When the sickly feeling finally dissipates, it is quickly replaced by intense hunger. My hollow stomach growls, and I rack my brain, trying to think about when I consumed anything other than Ambrosia. I can't think of anything, though; the Ambrosia staved off all symptoms of hunger. In my superhuman state, I transcended the need to eat. Or so I thought.

With my sweat-slick cheek pressed against the cool porcelain surface of the toilet, I don't feel so godlike anymore.

When my stomach finally settles, I lie on the floor of the defunct shower and try to sleep. I'm half-awake when the body aches begin. My overworked muscles are heavy, swollen, raw with pain. I lie on my back, paralyzed, subject to the rhythmic, agonizing throbbing of my limbs, which only intensifies as the moments pass. Before long, it feels like a fire is blazing beneath my skin. I whimper in agony, wishing not for the first time that I could crawl out of my own feeble body.

Despite this torment and my faltering defiance, my plan is working. Slowly but surely, my memories are returning.

Jace. How he cheated on me, how he'd verbally and emotionally abused me. How I let him break me down. How he died, too blinded by the anger and disgust he held for me to notice he tore through a red light, only to get T-boned by another car.

I'd be better off not thinking about how my parents wrote me off as a failure for not finishing school like they had, for never living up to their expectations. For moving in with Jace in the first place. For getting pregnant.

Better off not thinking about how when grief and guilt had walled me in, I wasn't able to bring myself to call my own family.

Because they were right. They were right all along. They tried to warn me. I ignored them. And now they want nothing to do with me. They weren't even there for me when he died.

The abhorrent memories flash before me like the scenes from the TV screens Rory showed me long ago. I remember how Rory held me, how he told me it was okay to forget.

"It's okay... I don't blame you..."

It had felt so good to forget. I close my eyes and remember the sweet oblivion resulting from losing memory after memory.

Just when I manage to clear my mind of awful memories for one brief moment, I look up and see the toilet. Seeing it triggers a painful feeling deep in my chest, but at first, I don't know why. All at once, I'm overcome by nausea, and my chest tightens, signaling an oncoming panic attack.

I remember going to the yoga studio to drown out a traumatic experience.

No, no, no... I know what's coming now. I can feel the memory violently thrashing to my conscious mind like a drowning victim, demanding to be acknowledged.

Me, on the toilet, my gut twisted up in pain.

Me, crying over the pool of blood that was our baby.

Me, feeling the hope die in my chest.

Overwhelmed by the buried memory, I pull my knees up to my chest and bury my head in them. I try hard not to think of my miscarriage, but it washes over me as if tired of being ignored.

I don't think I can do this.

It's then that I remember Gideon and how Mount Olympus finally sucked him in. The water fountain.

There isn't one in here, but there is a sink, a shower, a toilet. Ambrosia could be flowing through the entire piping system here. I hate myself for even considering giving up, and part of me thinks the idea is ludicrous. But my aching body and my despondent mind demand that I at least check.

Just one sip.

Dragging myself to my feet, I crawl to the sink and twist the handle with a tremulous hand.

And nothing comes out. Not even water.

I wait, my thirst intensifying with every moment. Panic grips my heart, and I stumble back to the shower in the opposite corner of the room, nearly wrenching the handles off the walls as I try it again. Still nothing.

That only leaves me with the toilet. The idea of sticking my head into the porcelain bowl sickens me, but it's my only option. I know by now I'm dehydrated. My tongue sticks to the roof of my mouth, and my lips are chapped.

But there's still the layer of strident yellow vomit in the toilet. I flush it down and prepare myself to do the unthinkable.

The bowl doesn't refill after sucking away my sickness.

"What?" My voice is hoarse as I grip the bowl with both hands and gape at its emptiness.

And I swear I can hear mocking laughter from outside the bathroom door.

"What am I doing?" I wrench myself away from the toilet bowl, backing into the wall.

The sound of laughter snakes into my tired mind, reviving the defiance I displayed when the staff gave me their ultimatum.

I look at the door, thinking, *There's plenty of Ambrosia out there. I could...*

"No!" I curl into a ball and let the laughter strengthen my resolve. I dig my nails into my skin, my nails leaving curved imprints on my arms. "I can't go back."

* * *

The craving passes gradually. The agony, however, continues to rage throughout my body.

This is Hell... I'm in Hell!

The thought is punctuated by stabbing pain in my head. I crawl to the other side of the room and switch off the light. The darkness provides little relief from the headaches at first, but I lie on the tiled ground and wait for the pain to go away. I try to force myself to calm down, but I feel as though I'm steadily coming unhinged. Losing it.

"Hell..." The word feels funny on my tongue, especially considering that time in the pool when I compared this place to Heaven itself. Nirvana. Pure bliss. I laugh, a sound so crazed and hysterical that it hardly sounds like it belongs to me. I'm frightened by the sound.

With the water cut off, though, I can't help but feel a strange sense of comfort, knowing that there's nothing I can do. I've got no choice but to live with the decision I've made to get clean. At this point, I'm too exhausted to walk out the door, and definitely too weak and frightened to face whoever waits beyond it. This is it. I'm either going to make it out of this hellhole barely alive or die from Ambrosia withdrawals. Either way, all that's left to do is wait.

It shouldn't be long. I doubt I have much time. My breaths come in more shallow by the second, and my throat is sandpaper-parched from dehydration.

All of a sudden, a loud scraping sound like metal against stone echoes in the room. Fluorescent light floods in from the corridor—the door has been pushed open. I instinctively shut my eyes, but someone flips the bathroom light switch. My head pounds once more as I force my eyes open and face the intruder.

A sharply dressed young man steps into my bathroom and closes the steel door behind him. With a great deal of effort, I drag myself as far away from him as I can as he faces me and crouches to my level as if about to talk to a small child.

It's odd seeing him dressed this way—looking more like a hotshot CEO than the fitness enthusiast I knew him as. But his gray eyes, honey-blond hair, and crooked smile give him away instantly. Rory.

"Not my real name, you know," he says, and I can almost feel him rooting around in my addled mind like it seems he's done so many times before. "I have another: Valmath."

I have never heard the name before, but somehow, those two syllables fill me with unspeakable dread as soon as they're spoken, as if they signal the end of the world. Or at least my world. No sooner than they're uttered, I'm cold, trembling, unable to meet his gaze.

I swallow hard and force the words to come out. "W-where am I, then?"

His lips curl in a cruel smile. "Well, you're not in Hell. At least, not yet."

My head snaps up in shock. "What's that supposed to mean?"

He shakes his head, his steely eyes boring into me. "You're smart enough. Tell me: what do you *know* to be true?" He reaches over and laces my hair around his fingers, making my head sway. I grimace, thinking of the clip I'd watched of Rory's father dragging his son up by the hair. That scene had troubled me, had made me empathetic toward Rory—Valmath. I can't reconcile that memory with the way he's acting now.

"Come on!" Valmath pulls my hair hard, making me cry out. "Any wild theories rolling around in that little brain of yours?"

His touch, which once filled me with such comfort, now makes me feel unclean. Defiled. I want to yank my head out of his hand, but I'm paralyzed by fear, bewildered at this change in Rory.

"Well?" He releases my hair, but his tone is sharp with impatience. "Go on."

I don't want to say it. It seems silly, but everything within me tells me it's the truth, nonetheless. "You... You're not from this world?"

His silence dares me to continue. What little courage I have left melts away under the intensity of his merciless stare.

"I don't know...d-demon?" It's a struggle getting the word out, and I feel no relief once I've spoken it. My face flushes, and I feel almost foolish for suggesting it, half-expecting Valmath to fall into a fit of mocking laughter at my stupid ideas.

But no. Instead, Valmath claps his hands a few times. "See? Smart girl."

Immediately, I slide my hand under my shirt to grip the silver cross hanging around my neck. For a split second, I consider taking it out and holding it in front of his face like they do in the movies, but before I have the chance, the mocking laughter finally does come.

"Really?" He raises a brow, his laugh sending chills straight down to my bones. "*That's* the route you're going for? Adorable."

I release the cross, shame making my cheeks burn.

He crouches in front of me. I smell something like a mixture of sulfur and mint on his breath as he says, "See, I'm not just a demon. Far from it. I'm something of an innovator among my peers." He smirks, eyes distant. "Too smart and too creative for Hell, and don't let anyone tell you otherwise once you get there."

My heartbeat is so frantic that I'm sure Valmath can hear it. He winks at me, clearly relishing in my terror.

"So dear old Dad kicked me out," he continues. "Something about 'issues with authority.'" He makes quotation marks in the air with his fingers.

My stomach does somersaults. A demon bad enough to have been kicked out of Hell?

"It was rough at first, wandering the earth aimlessly, alone. But then I had an epiphany: Now I have time. So much time!" Valmath's eyes light up with childlike glee. "So I did what I love to do best: screw with humans. Making cursed objects that slowly consume their lives. Creating plagues that stump even the best doctors. Turning their own homes into their personal prisons. All kinds of fun stuff." His eyes twinkle at the sadistic memories. Seeing his brazen, sadistic glee over the host of lives he has ruined makes every hair on my body stand on end. The moment passes, and his countenance darkens.

"But you know. No one can stay isolated forever." He sits cross-legged across from me on the tile floor. "You know that. Nothing worse than being kicked out of home. Even when your home is literal Hell."

He places a hand on my knee as he leans in closer, his eyes wild. His touch fills me with a chilling sensation like that of bugs crawling all over my skin. I want nothing more than to wrench myself free, but I can't bring myself to move.

"So I'm going home," the demon continues. "But I'm no fool. I know better than to come back empty-handed. Dad has this nasty tendency to hold grudges, but even he can't resist a good, old-fashioned sacrifice.

I figured, a couple thousand freshly harvested human souls ought to do the trick."

Disgusted, I glare at him. "So those videos in the security room? How did you—"

He shakes his head. "I just took bits and pieces of other people's sob stories and pasted my face onto them." He laughs. "Shit, I even took one or two details from your own life, just to mess with you. Not like you would have noticed or cared. You were so desperate to connect with me, so obsessed with the idea that someone like me could love someone like you." He cracks a mocking smile. "Pathetic, really."

I start to protest but can't bring myself to form the words. My cheeks burn as the truth of Valmath's words sinks in.

Valmath scoots himself toward me, so close that our shoulders touch. I want to push him away, but I'm paralyzed with fear. He smiles and inhales deeply as if my fear emits a pleasant aroma.

"What happens now?" As soon as I ask the question, I wish I hadn't. He claps me on the shoulder, hard. "Well, once I've harvested a hundred or so more souls, I finally get to leave this miserable planet."

He strokes my cheek. I push him away, but he grabs me by the shoulders, digging his fingernails into my skin.

"After we get back, what becomes of you is none of my concern." He relaxes his grip but tilts his head closer to my ear. He whispers, "I could give you an idea, but I wouldn't want to spoil the fun."

When Valmath stands, I can finally breathe freely. He brushes off his clothes, stuffs his hands in his pockets, then nods once in lieu of a goodbye before turning toward the door.

With some effort, I manage to stand, holding the sink with one hand for support.

"Wait!"

He turns back toward me, one eyebrow arched.

"Just... Why? I mean, why me?" As I ask the question, it sounds pitiful to me. Whiny, even. But I don't care. I have to know.

"Why you?"

"What did I do to deserve this? What did any of us do?" I remember Gideon, who was just trying to find his brother. I remember Sadie, who was dying to hear from her estranged daughter. Countless people who had families and stories and futures until some self-serving demon played their weaknesses against them. Against me.

He rolls his silver eyes. "Deserve?" He removes his hand from the doorknob, crossing his arms. "Oh, right, because you're so damned special. Because you must have been 'destined' for this, right?" He sucks his teeth. "Humans. Always thinking they're 'the chosen one,' whether for good or for ill."

I shake my head, dissatisfied. My mind can't fathom the idea that there's no rhyme or reason for my ending up here.

Probably still reading my thoughts, Valmath continues. "You really want to know how you ended up here? Well, here it is: I enjoy human suffering, and yours *called* to me."

I stare at him, dumbfounded.

He leans against the wall, arms crossed. "Yes, I know. You never actually summoned a demon to take you into a pocket universe," he says with an almost casual shrug. "But you simply *radiated* misery. Always thinking, 'If only this,' and 'If only that.' I could smell the 'if onlys' from a mile away, and I knew it'd be easy. I gave you everything you wanted, and you wandered right into my trap like a good little sheep."

I want to protest, but I know I can't. Once again, he's right. The bastard is right.

"Please!" Tears spring to my eyes and blur my vision as the words leave my mouth. "I don't want to die! I don't want to go to…" I can't bring myself to say the word "Hell." Saying it makes it a reality.

The wicked smile creeps back up Valmath's face and chills me to my core. He turns the doorknob.

What if I leave? Even though I still have to lean against a sink for support, even though my aching legs can barely support me, I can't help but wonder what would happen if I tried making a break for it. Do I stand a chance?

"You want to try to make a run for it? Knock yourself out. That could be fun. For me." He opens the door and stands halfway in the corridor. "Or stay in here and rot in your own vomit. Also fun. But rest assured, Crystal." Here, his voice drops an octave in pitch, to the point where he hardly sounds human anymore. "No matter what you choose, the outcome will be the same: You'll be mine forever. You've got less than half a soul as it stands, and you'll not leave this place until I have it all."

I want more than anything to be strong, but I can't stop the sob from escaping my throat.

Valmath takes another backward step into the corridor. "Oh, by the way, in case you do decide to leave, I've...redecorated the gym since you've been in here. I've got a feeling you won't like it." The demon chuckles.

Can't stop myself from whining as I reach out and plead, "Please, just let me go! I want to go home!"

He cocks an eyebrow. "No, you really don't. That's the problem."

He slips into the corridor and shuts the door behind him. My legs finally give out on me. I crumple to the ground, shaking, crying.

Weak.

Chapter 17

After that encounter, time seems even more muddled. I'm caught in one droning, harrowing moment of isolation—too weak to stand, too afraid to make myself leave the bathroom and face whatever lies beyond the steel door. Every breath, every movement is punctuated by stabbing pain. Every second of sleep, plagued by vivid, feverish nightmares.

The body that I worshiped with such fervor is turning itself against me like it always does. I wonder how long I have left.

I sit with my back against the cool tile wall, head buried between my knees, sweat pouring from my brow. My teeth knock together as my body is wracked with tremors.

Curiosity gets the better of me. I grab hold of the bathroom sink and use it to hoist myself up on my aching legs. Holding the porcelain sink for support, I look at my reflection; the sight of my pale skin, the shadows underneath my red-rimmed eyes, my unruly dark curls—all framed by the strange angles and softening muscles I've developed through tireless exercise—the sight makes me sick to my stomach. Cold on the inside and out.

I can almost feel death's shadow over me, making the nape of my neck tingle.

When I see a dark shape through the mirror, standing by the door, it takes me a long moment to process its existence. Fear doesn't strike me but rather rolls over me in waves, making the already frigid room feel at least ten degrees colder. Slowly, tentatively, I turn around and face the shape, still gripping the sink with one hand as my knees knock together.

The longer I stare at the figure, the more the shadows disappear from around it. Gradually, recognition sets in, and my terror is replaced by sorrow.

The figure is short, cross-armed. Wears thick-rimmed glasses and runs a hand through his salt-and-pepper hair, shaking his head disdainfully at me.

"...Dad?"

His deep-set eyes don't meet mine. Hearing my voice, his scowl deepens.

"Dad, please..." My lip begins to quiver.

He holds up his hands, stopping my plea in its tracks. Turns his back on me.

"Dad, help me, please!"

Just when his countenance begins to soften, another figure appears next to him: a short woman with a shock of red hair hanging to her shoulders. Julia.

She says nothing to Dad. Her presence is enough to strengthen his resolve. He crosses his arms again, making his button-down shirt tighten over his stocky frame.

My vision goes blurry with tears. "Dad..."

Julia tightens her jaw. "You got yourself into this mess. You deserve this."

She disappears through the closed door, and Dad follows behind her, without a backward glance in my direction. Alone again, I allow myself to collapse into another bout of crying.

$$* * *$$

It's the first of many hallucinations resulting from my Ambrosia withdrawals. Sometimes I hear voices, horrible grating whispers muttering words I can't understand or half understand. Voices echoing Valmath's chilling words. *Half a soul...* Sometimes I see monstrous shapes, demonic figures that I never would have imagined my mind could conjure up. Sometimes when I'm in that uncanny valley between sleep and wakefulness, a sudden sound will jolt me awake—a crash or a scream or some familiar voice calling my name. But when I awaken, sometimes slamming my head hard against the tile in the process, there's never anyone there.

Another voice comes to me—sharp, bitter, garbled. Jace's.

Dread claws along the edges of my mind. *No... Not you!*

I can feel myself floating toward consciousness, and I struggle to stay asleep. It's useless, though. Before long, I open my eyes and pin myself against the wall as my mind grapples with what it is seeing.

He's standing in front of the door, his back turned toward me, looking just as he did that night he left. His hands are stuffed in his pockets, and I can see them ball up beneath the denim of his jeans.

When my heart begins to race, I tell myself over and over, *Not real, he's not real.* And at the same time, I want to call out to him. I want to kick him, curse at him, fall into his arms, and weep. In the end, all I can manage is to squeak out his name. "Jace?"

He looks up to the ceiling, crossing his arms. He doesn't turn to face me, but my gut wrenches when I hear him mutter, "Maybe if you weren't such a fat pig..."

Something snaps within me. Despite my exhaustion and pain, I'm on my feet, hands clenched and poised to strike.

And then he turns to face me.

He changes.

I'm close enough to smell his cologne when he turns around. His mouth is twisted in an anguished expression, his eyes swollen shut.

Shards of glass protrude from his neck, his cheek, his left eye. A wound gapes like a monstrous mouth in his head, and blood flows freely, coating his entire body like a second skin.

I try to cry out, but my throat closes up to choke the sound. My body spasms as I'm caught between the desire to catch Jace's wounded body before it falls and the need to clamber as far away from him as possible. In my moment of hesitation, he falls forward, his mangled body landing on mine. I'm covered in his blood. Screaming, I fight to free myself from his weight, but I'm too weak, and every movement results in pangs in my overworked muscles. At last, I slide out from beneath him, but a long glass shard catches me in the arm, shredding my skin as I try to get away. Blood flowing, I crawl backward until I hit a wall on the other end of the room.

Jace's blood pools around him, flowing into the grooves between each of the tiles.

I want to look away, but I can't. Tears stream down my cheeks as I stare at the body, and I hear the distant howling of police sirens. Three soft knocks echo on the door.

"No, no, no, no…" I curl up into the fetal position, shaking uncontrollably, pressing my hand against the wound in my upper arm. I close my eyes.

Breathe, I tell myself. It takes some effort, but I'm able to slow my breathing, even as my heart continues to race.

I can still smell the pooling blood. I keep my eyes shut.

To my own surprise, I smile.

Because there's something cathartic about the experience, like ripping off a bandage from a festering wound. Like looking straight in the face of the undead beast whose howling has haunted my nightmares. Not killing it yet but acknowledging its existence.

A spark of strength lights up in my chest—not enough to fight or do anything useful, but just enough to make me open my eyes. When I do, the body disappears. The knocking sounds cease. The blood—both his blood and mine—vanishes, but I still feel its sticky residue. I can still smell it in the air.

"Gone." In my time here, I've seen visions come and go, and I've simply endured them. Waited them out as a hapless victim to my mind's wild imaginings.

This one was different, though; I know somehow, it was Valmath pulling the strings, crafting that gory nightmare creature with just enough horrific detail to weaken me.

And it had worked for a while. But then something changed.

Something has changed. At the moment, though, I'm not able to put a finger on what that is. Instead, I shut my eyes, letting relief wash over me, slowing my heart rate and shutting off the adrenaline flow in my veins. I know I haven't seen the last of these hallucinations, but for now, I take comfort in the fact that I somehow managed to will one away.

* * *

Once I've calmed down, I spend a good while processing my encounter with undead Jace. For the first time since quitting Ambrosia, I'm proud of myself. But I don't know if I can repeat this success next time one of Valmath's visions comes crawling back.

I reach into my shirt and fidget with my cross necklace like I've done so often during times of anxiety. This time, though, I don't let go when the memory begins to form, shadowy and incomplete. This time, I let all the warm confusion of love well up within me as I remember how I used to be. How love was once a warm blanket I settled under night after night. How once, someone slipped the chain around my neck, whispering words of comfort in my ear. How someone kissed me goodnight and told me tomorrow would be better.

The nostalgia quickly turns to rage, though, as I remember what came next. The new wife and her constant criticism. The arguments. The feeling of never being enough. That final confrontation when I left home, never to return, carrying the pain of my rejection with me like a heavy suitcase.

I squeeze the cross so hard, it leaves an imprint on my palm. Dodging from these painful memories has been my lifestyle for so long. It's what got me to stay so long in Mount Olympus in the first place. Sure, there was the allure of seemingly effortless weight loss, but it was the feeling of being unburdened by my confusing past that truly drew me in.

But look where that got me.

I release the pendant, putting my head in my hands. For the first time in a long, long time, I don't want to simply pretend that the bad things in my life never happened to me. I don't want to push down my baggage into the dark of my mind.

For once, I want something more. Something harder.

I want to get better.

But when I look at the door, it feels so far away. The very thought of making the long trek back home, not to mention facing whatever trials Valmath has lined up for me, makes the pain in my limbs intensify. Reminds me of my weakness and my sleep deprivation.

I *need* to get better.

But as my physical fragility wars against my defiant mind, all I can do is pray that I'm not too late.

Chapter 18

Time flows on, meandering like muddy water, wild and unchecked. I try counting the minutes, but I can never keep them straight. I'm too tired and foggy to keep it up for very long. It's hard enough differentiating between reality from my feverish imaginings. Eventually, I give up trying, surrendering to the bizarre hallucinations that play out before me like low-quality films.

Little by little, memories continue to return, lighting up my addled mind like stars in the dark canvas of night. The bad thoughts came first, probably because they were the ones that I was fixating on before coming to Mount Olympus. Eventually, good memories return too, but only in snippets. Compared to the bad memories, these are choppy, incomplete.

Someone picks me up in strong arms, whirling me around while I scream with delight.

I careen downhill on a bike, fighting to keep myself steady while someone cheers me on.

Someone slips a silver necklace around my neck, whispering words of comfort.

I keep twisting and fiddling with the necklace, pressing it hard against my fingertips as I grapple with the fragmented memories. I remember approaching Rory—Valmath—once and asking him if my life outside these walls was worth it, and all he showed me were the reasons that it wasn't. Now that happy memories are so disjointed, so fractured and so infrequent, I begin to wonder again if this was a mistake. It would be so easy to walk out and turn myself into Valmath. I'd be all right, so long as I kept taking the Ambrosia and tried not to question my surroundings too much.

But when I fidget with my necklace, I take a deep breath and try to push aside the doubts.

"Just hold on a little longer," I tell myself. "Maybe there's something worthwhile out there."

* * *

After a while, sleep comes more easily and is less frequented by trippy nightmares than it was before. The headaches and chills gradually go away, though my body still feels weak. I let out a bitter, single-syllable laugh; all this time, I thought my incessant exercise was strengthening me, and now the mere thought of walking down a hallway exhausts me.

Unable to do much of anything else, I wait for my memories to return. The fragments of good memories—so beautiful even in their brokenness—fill me with insatiable desire, a need to piece together the puzzle they lay out before me.

Because if I can, I'll have a reason to face whatever lies beyond that door.

I'm sitting with my back against the concrete wall, staring at the door separating me from the idyllic Hell I left behind. My time of addiction feels distant and hazy, like a nightmare. As I ponder the bright memory shards, I'm sickened when I realize how foolish I've been: I wanted to throw my entire life away and replace it with a poor imitation.

"That's a heavy burden to bear..." Rory—Valmath— had said. *"I don't blame you..."*

I scoff. "I'm so stupid," I say aloud, thinking of how easy it was for me to fall prey to the demon's trap. How willingly I succumbed to Valmath's honeyed words. But even now, my heart drops when I think of the trauma I had come to Mount Olympus to escape from.

Regardless, I know better. In my heart of hearts, I know it's time to move on, even if I don't know how. All this time I spent trying to outrun my demons. Maybe it's time I learned to face them.

The pain in my head has reduced to a dull, continual throb, like a heartbeat. My stomach is free from nausea, but it twists up in hunger. My throat is rough and dry like crumpled paper, parched with thirst. Worst of all are the continual aches and pains resulting from any slight movement—a sign that I've worked my body beyond its limits, and it's finally paying me back for my foolishness.

Every fiber of my body demands that I stay still, not leave. I know it will be too hard, too painful.

But the fuzzy memories do their work, slowly, gently. Despite the messiness of my life, they show me that there's someone out there who cares for me. That there must be hope, however small, that things can get better. That I can get better.

And I know one thing: I'm not getting better in this bathroom.

Before long, I can't take it anymore. I want to raise myself off the cold tile floor, open the door, and into a wild sprint toward freedom. The very thought of standing makes my head swim. And even though I know the door was locked from the inside, I know there's probably someone waiting out there to greet me as soon as I make a move.

Valmath's haunting warning echoes in my mind: *"You've got less than half a soul as it stands, and you will not leave this place until I have all of it."*

I shudder, almost able to feel the hollowness of my half-soul rattling within me.

There's no other way. I've never considered myself a brave person, but I have to try. I can't just lie down on this cold floor and die. Even if it means dying out there.

With a great deal of effort, I roll over, grab the edge of the sink and use it to hoist myself up. At last, I'm standing on my wobbly legs like a newborn foal. Before opening the door, I catch a glimpse of myself in the mirror and see how my body transformed during my self-imposed incarceration. I'm no longer frighteningly athletic. No, instead, I'm skinny. Too skinny. I'm pale, gaunt, fragile. I can't bear to look any longer, but I can't bear the thought of leaving the bathroom either. After a moment's hesitation, I take a deep breath, shut my eyes, and push open the door.

The open door lets in a chilly draft that makes the hair on my arms stand on end. Opening my eyes, I'm baffled as I take in the unfamiliar scene laid out before me. And then I remember Valmath's words before he left my bathroom-cell: *"I've redecorated... you won't like it."*

He's done more than redecorate. He's fully transformed his master-piece.

This new version of Mount Olympus is desolate. No staff, no ever-smiling gym members. Not a soul in sight. The corridor is uncharac-teristically dark, only lit by a few ghostly green emergency lights along the wall.

The upbeat, thumping music has gone dead too, and the silence that has taken its place makes me uneasy. I take tentative steps, not knowing which direction to head in because everything looks so foreign in the dark. As I head toward what I'm pretty sure is the right direction toward the front door, I keep expecting someone to leap out of the shadows and seize me—and I know if that does happen, I won't have the strength to fight them off.

As I tiptoe through the dark corridor, the pain in my shins punctuating each step, I feel as though I've wandered into some bizarre alternate reality. The layout of the building I walk through is the same as it was when I first locked myself in the bathroom. It feels as though the building has been skinned of its former glory and dressed in the equivalent of sackcloth and ashes.

At last, I come to a door I didn't notice before, a heavy steel door like the one to the bathroom I hid in. A bright green "exit" sign shines above it, and another sign has the words "emergency exit" emblazoned on it. My heart flutters. *Could it really be that easy?*

I push the heavy door open and brace myself for an alarm to sound. The only sound I hear is that of the steel scraping against the concrete floor. I expect the smell of fresh air to waft through the door, to see the sun, to feel grass beneath my feet. But what I see instead is total darkness. I hear a howling sound, like that of distant, tormented spirits.

I hesitate, my trembling fingers wrapped around the cold doorknob as I stare into the abyss, then look back to the corridor from which I came. It's bad enough that I've been lured into Mount Olympus by my own stupidity. I don't want to walk headlong into another trap.

"Less than half a soul..." Valmath had said. *"Less than half a soul..."*

I replay the cryptic words in my mind, trying to make sense of them. Really, on a certain level, I know exactly what Valmath meant. But there's a part of me that doesn't want to accept that it's true.

I can't leave yet.

No. I have to take back what's mine. Even if it means playing right into his hands.

Trembling all over, I step through the doorway. Almost instantly, the door slams behind me, cutting out what little light I have. The distant chorus of howls echoes in my ears, plaintive and haunting.

When my quaking fingers find the cool surface of a concrete wall, I walk on.

This is insane! my mind screams. *I'm too weak to face him.*

But I walk on anyway.

* * *

Ignoring the fearful clamor in my head as I stumble through the dark, I press on... It's even harder ignoring the fiery pain that accompanies every step I make through the dark passageway; it's like my muscles are embedded with knife blades, and every step drives them deeper into my body.

But I keep moving, leaning on the wall for support with one hand while stretching my other arm out in front of me to make sure I don't walk into anything. Just when my heartbeat begins to settle down, I feel a slight pressure against the arm that's holding the wall, like the concrete is pushing against me.

Like the wall is moving.

Stop it! I tell myself. *You're being paranoid.*

But then my left shoulder brushes against something cold and solid—concrete. My fingers fumble over the concrete to make sure, and that's when I feel the other wall brushing my right shoulder.

I break into a sprint, but with the Ambrosia having worn off, each step is torture. I grit my teeth as the knife-blade sensation accompanies every clumsy stride. My chest heaves as I feel the pressure from the walls edging closer, closer. In my panicked mind, a gory image of my body exploding like a water balloon between the walls plays and replays, and my desperate screaming of, "God, please, please, no," echoes down the corridor.

When I run headlong into a steel door at the end of the hall, the walls are close enough that I have to stand sideways. My hands fumble over the cold, dark metal for the handle. *No, no, no...the handle is gone, the wall crushed it—and I'm next.*

But when my shaking fingers find the unmarred handle at last, I release a crazed laugh. There is just enough room for me to turn it and push the door open, tumbling out of the perilous corridor just before the walls slam together. I collapse, falling to the floor on my hands and knees. My body is spent, my soul—what's left of it—shaken by the harrowing experience.

As much as I want to lie on the ground and cry until there are no more tears left to shed, I will myself to get to my feet. It takes everything within me to keep my knees from giving way under me as I stand and examine my surroundings.

I've stumbled into a vast room, dimly illuminated by what looks like the light from aquarium tanks. All around me, windows line the walls, but the light streaming through them is too bright to be daylight.

Or maybe I've just forgotten what daylight looks like.

With some effort, I stand, holding the concrete wall for support until my sore legs stop trembling. With heavy feet, I venture farther into the wide, empty room, drawn in by the strange lights. As I draw nearer to the lighted windows, my vision blurs; the light is almost too much to comprehend after being in the dark for so long. I blink rapidly, approaching one of the windows with its ghostly glow.

"What the...?" I squint, walking closer. A chill rocks through my body as I try to make sense of what I'm seeing.

There's something behind each of the windows. Figures bobbing lightly in their watery prisons, feet hovering above the ground. Eyes closed as if in rest, mouths half-open.

The realization makes me freeze mid-step, but I can't make myself stop staring at the figures, at their expressionless faces.

Because I know these faces. I know them all.

I've seen them sprinting down the walking track, flying up and down the climbing wall, diving into the pool.

Valmath's prisoners.

My heart races, but my breathing seems to stop altogether. I want to run, but terror makes my legs forget how to work.

That is, until one of the figures catches my attention. I see it in my periphery: dark skin, short stature, ill-fitting Mount Olympus attire hanging on his wiry frame.

"Gideon." I hobble toward him, wincing with every step, pressing my face against the glass of his case. It is him. It's strange seeing him like this, the perpetually worried expression replaced by one of apparent rest. But the longer I examine him, the more agitated he appears. His limbs float at an awkward angle, and his mouth quirks now and again.

He's sleeping, but not resting.

He's stuck in a nightmare he can't awaken himself from.

A nightmare within a nightmare.

As I ponder Gideon's predicament, the hair on the nape of my neck suddenly stands on end. The blood drains from my face, my body alerting me of another's presence before my eyes can register the figure standing a few feet away from me, just out of my periphery.

I whip my body around so fast, I nearly topple over. I'm greeted by a familiar face.

"Crystal." Clarissa's grin gleams wickedly, catching the light from the aquarium tanks. "I knew you'd come around."

She looks just as I remember her. Diminutive in stature. Dark hair streaked with strands of silver. Overall, non-threatening in appearance. But there's something unsettling about her presence. Maybe it's because this is the first time I've seen her not carrying her free sample tray. Maybe it's her shit-eating grin.

Clarissa steps toward me, hands behind her back. She glances at the bodies behind the glass as she approaches, and I swear that she's growing taller with every step. I try to stand firm, but when she gets too close, I instinctively step away, clenching and unclenching my fists to keep them from trembling.

"What is this place?" I ask, unable to look at her.

"This?" She gestures at the wall of prisoners. "Isn't it obvious?"

I have a few ideas, but my frightened mind doesn't want to entertain them.

Clarissa ceases closing in on me and, instead, approaches one of the glass cases, placing a hand on it, almost tenderly. "Poor saps give up after a while. After working themselves to the bone, after surrendering most of their souls...they just drop. So we bring them here, where we can finish the job."

I glance up at the body behind the glass, and my stomach knots up when I realize I recognize him. Tall. Muscular. Eagle tattoo. Elijah, I remember. So this is where he went when he disappeared.

Clarissa turns back toward me with that skin-split smirk. I nearly jump out of my skin when I realize I was right earlier: she *is* growing in height. At this point, the top of her head is almost close enough to brush against Elijah's chin.

I want to bolt away from her, but a familiar scent makes me freeze up all over again: cigarette smoke.

All at once, I realize where I am, and I instinctively glance toward the corner of the room where the strange old man should be. Sure enough, there he is, still oblivious to the danger surrounding him. Still blowing cigarette smoke into the air as he crouches against the wall.

Clarissa notices me staring. Eyes burning, she snaps, "What are you looking at?"

"N-nothing..."

Just when I consider asking if she knows who the old man is, Clarissa whips around, shooting a murderous glance in the direction of the old man. He disappears as if she willed him away. Turning back to face me, she sets her jaw. "What did you see?"

It's then that the gears in my frantic mind slow down, processing Clarissa's strong reaction. I let the fading smell of cigarettes keep me grounded. *Remember me,* the odor seems to whisper. *I'm important.*

Clarissa snaps her fingers in my face. "Hello? I asked you a question."

Play dumb, I tell myself. "Nothing. I was just confused... What did you mean by 'finish the job'?"

Clarissa emits a one-note laugh, shaking her head, which only seems to speed up her inhuman growth. Her eyes gleam wickedly, but the tension in her demeanor has melted away. Maybe she bought my feigned innocence. "You know what it means," she says. "I know Valmath spoke to you. You just can't accept the fact that your soul is forfeit." She turns and points to Elijah. "Just like his."

I take a backward step, unable to keep from picturing myself behind that glass, helpless, drowning as my soul is sucked away from me. I can't let her see me afraid, though. I set my jaw and plant my feet, even as my mind is screaming, *Think, think, think, do something*, even as the cigarette smell fades away entirely, before I can make sense of its significance.

"I've redecorated..." The words echo over and over in my memory, demanding my attention.

I clutch my necklace, forcing myself to breathe. "I won't let you have me."

Clarissa raises an eyebrow. "Ah. So, what, you're strong now?" She sucks her teeth. "You have no idea what strength is, girl."

I start to protest, but something happens—the lights from the coffin-tanks flicker, bathing the whole room with darkness momentarily. But in the dark, Clarissa's silver eyes shine like those of a lioness skulking in the shadows. Predator's eyes.

I turn to run away from her, but I'm too slow. She catches me by both arms, sharp nails digging into my skin as I struggle. I kick and try to wrench myself out of her grip, but it's useless. With seemingly no effort at all, she pushes me toward the wall.

Toward the tanks.

"Still feeling strong, girl?" Her nails sink deeper into my skin, making me whimper.

Focus! The way out is right in front of me, but fear obscures everything like a dense fog.

Glancing behind me, I see an empty tank directly in my path. She's guiding me toward it.

No!

I drop to the ground, going boneless, forcing her hands open just enough for me to break out. My freedom is short-lived, though. As I'm attempting to crawl away, she snags me by the ankle and drags me back, then grabs my hair by the roots and forces me upward. I cry out, flailing limbs frantically trying to strike her somewhere, anywhere.

There it is again. The smell of smoke. I glance past Clarissa just long enough to catch a glimpse of the old man again. Shaking, I muster the courage to face Clarissa, hoping against all hope that she doesn't notice my looking away.

Breathe, I coach myself. *Think. Focus!*

"Who do you think you are?" She's inches away from my face, and her foul, hot breath makes me grimace. "How dare you challenge a servant of Valmath?"

With one powerful motion, she shoves me backward. My head cracks against something hard, making my vision go white for a second—glass. I attempt to step away from the tank, but I can't move. My limbs lock into place like I'm being pinned down by an unseen hand.

Clarissa's eyes narrow as she closes in on me. She's now a full head taller than I am, and her arms bulge with newly-grown muscle. Her mouth twitches in a crazed smile as she puts both hands on the glass behind me.

I close my eyes and wait for her to strike, but something else happens. Something worse. The glass behind me begins to give way. Not cracking, though. It's *melting,* as if some strange force behind it is thinning the glass barrier and making it absorb me.

I'm being pulled into the tank.

Terrified, I try to thrash against the pressure holding me back, try to peel myself off the tank, but it's no use. Clarissa's wicked smile assures me of that much. Trying to move is like trying to wake myself from a sleep paralysis nightmare; every attempt seems to tighten the pressure weighing against me. My breaths come in gasps. My bones rattle beneath my skin as I attempt to wrench myself free.

"He said you might put up a fight," Clarissa says. "Didn't know you'd be this much fun."

"Yeah? Well, where is he, then?" I risk another glance toward the stranger in the corner, sifting through my cluttered thoughts to figure out why his presence seems to anchor me.

The glass continues to thin beneath me. I'm half-convinced that maybe this isn't part of Clarissa's design, that maybe when the glass entirely disappears, the water will knock Clarissa backward, providing me a means of escape. But deep down, I know better. I know somehow, once I'm in the tank, the glass will reform, trapping me inside, and flooding my lungs with water. Killing me.

Until then, let's see if I can make this bitch squirm.

"Where is he?" I repeat. "Why do *you* have to do his dirty work?"

She gestures around her. "Someone's got to keep this whole artifice running. Besides, what you call 'dirty work' proves to him I'm worthy."

The glass closes in on me, biting into my skin. I can feel the water beneath me, its chill making my skin crawl. "Worthy for what?" I spit. But I don't much care about her answer. I'm focusing on the smell of cigarettes.

It doesn't belong. He doesn't belong. Why is he here?

Clarissa straightens up, crossing her arms over her chest. "When Valmath rises to full power, I'll rise with him." A faraway look crosses her face. "He cut me a great deal." She shoots a mocking glance at me. "Far better than the one you signed up for."

The water crawls up my skin, making me wish I could jump out of my useless body and somewhere far, far away. "He's using you!" I shout, still looking over Clarissa's shoulder. "He's not even a full demon. He got...demoted."

Keep her talking, I tell myself. *Don't let her notice.*

"And?" Clarissa shrugs. "If he can pull off an illusion this elaborate without his full powers, imagine what he can do at full strength." She gestures around the room as if I'm supposed to be impressed by the empty darkness. "When Valmath rises, he's taking me with him." She fixes her gaze on me. "As long as I collect your soul."

Illusion... redecorated. I close my eyes tightly, blocking out everything in an effort to piece together the puzzle pieces Valmath has left for me.

As if doing so will keep me from sinking further into the tank.

I scan the room, glancing at the collection of soulless bodies before staring back toward the old man. "Why?" I ask, unable to keep the tremor out of my voice. "Why does he need my soul so badly?"

Why does this room feel familiar?

"Demons can't resist a struggle. Makes the victory that much more delicious." Clarissa takes a step toward me, putting a hand on my forehead. My flesh crawls at her touch. "Nice knowing you, Crystal."

I try to shake my head, but paralysis still locks up my joints. I want to scream, but fear makes my throat close up. The room spins.

I know this room!

The fog lifts. The final puzzle piece slides into place.

Too late.

With one swift motion, Clarissa pushes me under the water. The liquid glass closes in over me and solidifies, trapping me inside. Beyond it, Clarissa puts her hands in her pockets, a self-satisfied smirk on her face as she waits for me to die.

Chapter 19

Thirty seconds, I think to myself as I kick and punch the glass to no avail. *Thirty seconds is all I have before I run out of breath.*

Before I die.

My lungs scream for air. Even though I'm finally able to flail my limbs about, the pressure that hangs over my chest increases, tightening like a fist around my heart.

I swim to the top of the tank, fingers feeling along its ceiling to see if there's a gap between it and the water's surface—feeling for a small, merciful amount of air.

Nothing.

This is it. This is where I die.

The noose around my lungs tightens. I bang the glass repeatedly, uselessly.

Twenty seconds.

I open my eyes. Stare over Clarissa's shoulder. He's still there. Still nursing his cigarette.

Focus! My limbs relax even as my chest lights up with the agony of oxygen deprivation.

Mind over matter... I remember Rory's words as I fix my gaze on the old man who doesn't belong. The old man who managed to slip past Valmath's layers of illusion without even knowing it.

He's from my world, I tell myself. *The real world.*

It's why he's seemed so out of place. It's why Clarissa seemed so agitated when I noticed him.

Ten seconds.

I resist the urge to give into the panic that makes my heart thump irregularly—to ignore the way my lungs spasm, the way dark spots form along my periphery. My jaw locked tightly against the water, I press my hands against the glass and fix my gaze on the man—the tear in Valmath's illusion.

The way home.

Five seconds.

My body twitches as if electrocuted.

My head pounds.

Darkness takes me...Just as the glass begins to crack beneath my palms.

* * *

Three things happen all at once.

A skull-splitting shatter rings in my ears. I slam headfirst onto a concrete floor, water flattening me like a pancake against the rough surface. I feel shards of glass beneath my skin.

When the water ceases rushing over me, I gasp for air, rolling over on my back, ignoring the bite of glass shards.

I smell cigarette smoke and hear the shuffle of feet. Jumping up, I see the old man, his lit cigarette dropping from his fingers, staring at me with wide, terrified eyes.

It worked. My eyes well up with tears. *I've made it home. I know it.*

My relief is short-lived. Within seconds, I'm back in the tank-room, and the old man vanishes before my eyes. He's replaced by an enraged Clarissa, unnaturally tall and fist cocked to strike. I try to dodge her, but she catches me in the jaw, the bruising punch sending me hurtling to the ground.

"How?" She looms over me, poised to strike again.

I scoot backward, rifling through the broken glass.

Finally, my fingers close around the size and shape I'm looking for. Perfect.

Tucking the glass shard behind me, I grin at Clarissa. "You still believe in Valmath now?" I use one of the tanks to hoist myself up, swallowing the urge to wince from pain. "Looks like his illusion wasn't so perfect after all."

Clarissa's eyes flicker with uncertainty for a moment. But soon, her countenance hardens. Thick veins bulge on her forehead. "You don't know anything!"

My grip tightens around the shard. "Sounds like I know more than Val—"

Clarissa snaps. With a wild roar, she hurtles toward me, arms outstretched, ready to tear skin from bone. I'm ready for her. Waiting until she's within striking distance, I ram the glass into her abdomen twice. She's caught off guard as the blood begins to pour from the wound, stopping her charge and stepping back a few inches, gaping at the damage. Her brows knitted in equal parts horror and anger, she charges at me again, blood pouring from her stomach.

I run.

I'm too afraid to do anything else.

I don't have to run far, though. A wet, heavy thud echoes behind me, making me spin around in my tracks. I stop moving when I see Clarissa, face-first on the floor, a pool of blood blossoming around her. Her body twitches infrequently, and her fingers reach out as if still trying to reach me. The gory sight gives me immeasurable relief. That is until I hear her pitiful, whimpering cry: "Valmath..."

I half expect him to appear in a puff of smoke, to exact revenge on his loyal servant. The longer the silence stretches, the more uneasy I am.

My fingers tighten around the glass as I wait.

But he never shows.

When I finally allow myself to breathe, my relief gradually turns into anger. As Clarissa bleeds out, her still corpse shrinks back to its original size—a grim reminder of her humanity.

She wasn't a demon or a monster.

She was just a woman who had put her trust in a devil who had promised her the world, given her a fragment of his power, but then didn't even have the decency to defend her when it mattered most.

I set down the glass shard, my quivering hands sticky with Clarissa's blood. With halting steps, I approach the corpse. After tapping her lightly to ensure that she is, in fact, dead, I roll her body over. The smell of blood nearly knocks me off my feet, and one sight of the gaping wound makes the world tilt at a nauseating angle. The woman's eyes are open in a perpetual state of surprise and her colorless lips drawn slightly apart.

I killed her! The judgment rings loud and familiar in my head. I cover my mouth to stifle a sob, but the taste of blood makes me double over with nausea. Tears blind my vision, making Clarissa appear like nothing more than a mangled mass of flesh and blood. When I'm finally able to see clearly, I watch as the unnatural silver in Clarissa's eyes melts away, replaced by a gentle brown.

I reach down and close her eyes, and the tightness in my chest gradually fades. The nausea subsides, and the screaming in my brain settles to a dull roar. Snapping up straight, I reorient myself to my surroundings, reminding myself of the task ahead.

Turning around, I watch the collection of lifeless bodies bobbing in their glass prison cells. The guilt over Clarissa's slaying fades and is replaced by the memory of her sneer. Her violence. Her dedication to the entity that had made life a living nightmare for all these people.

For me.

I touch the surface of Gideon's tank, leaving behind a bloody hand-print. "Hold on, Gideon," I tell him. "I'm ending this. Now."

* * *

At last, this twisted version of Mount Olympus feels familiar. Knowing I came from a version of the weight room makes it easy to navigate to the lobby. The walk there is anything but easy, though.

The pain in my shins worsens, each labored step driving those imaginary knife-blades deeper into my bones. I'm sore, I'm exhausted, and I'm queasy as I replay the fight with Clarissa in my mind. I try not to think about how she looked, lying there, bleeding. Lifeless. But when I reach the hallway leading to the lobby—the one where she used to stand with her tray of little cups of Ambrosia—I want to vomit all over again. I hold the wall, waiting for the world to stop spinning.

Focus! You're almost there.

Almost home. Just one set of double doors separates me from freedom.

That is, once I find what I'm looking for first.

A familiar, saccharine voice interrupts my momentary respite. "Crystal!"

My head jerks up. Looking across the dark lobby, I see a single female figure seated at the front desk, her red hair shining in the warm glow of a solitary lamp. She swivels around in her office chair, her legs crossed as she files her perfect nails. The grin carved into her face gives way to her characteristic pout as she says, "You're not leaving already, are you?"

Chapter 20

For a moment, I'm paralyzed. Of course Sasha is still here after all this time, her little pout strangely unnerving in the glow of her desk lamp. Before Valmath told me the truth about Mount Olympus—before having to kill Clarissa—I would never have considered this chipper receptionist to be a threat. But I know better than to underestimate her now.

"What's the matter, darlin'?" She sets down her nail file, looking up at me with a fake innocent look that makes my skin crawl.

I take halting, hesitant steps toward her desk, my panicked mind trying to stitch together a half-decent idea of how to get into her files without being apprehended by her. At last, it comes to me.

"I need…Ambrosia…" I wheeze, imbuing every ounce of my exhaustion and pain I have into the words.

She looks me over, her steely eyes heavy with concern. "*I'll* say you do. You look like you've been hit by a train. What happened, sweetie?"

I nod. "Please," I beg, not about to explain where the blood on my clothes came from. I realize then that I'm playing a dangerous game. My request may be an attempt to get her to let her guard down, but from the moment I utter the name of my addiction, desire makes my heartbeat quicken. My mouth waters. My hands begin to shake.

Sasha cranes her head past me. "I wonder where Clarissa's run off to. Oh, well. I think I have some in the back. I won't be long." With that, she springs from her chair and disappears into the back office.

Now's my chance. Adrenaline kicks in, softening the pain as I clamber over Sasha's huge circular desk. For a moment, I try to sift through my jumbled memories to remember where exactly Sasha stored my registration file, but when I can't, I resort to pulling open every single filing drawer, trying hard not to make any noise, praying that none of them are locked.

Most of the drawers contain office supplies—when I come across a pair of scissors, I snatch it up and hide it in the waistband of my sweatpants. A replacement for the glass shard that I left in the weight room. To my mounting frustration, I find that some drawers are completely empty. *Come on! Where are they?*

I come to the last drawer. Locked. Of course it is. I stand to return to the desk, my hands fumbling over Sasha's belongings as I search for a key.

The sound of a door snapping open makes me jump. I whirl around to see Sasha, a bottle of Ambrosia in her hand and a cool, wicked grin on her face. Her free hand slides into the front pocket of her khakis and then produces a set of keys. Behind her, ghostly light from the security screens flickers behind her.

"Need something?" she says before pocketing the keys again.

She sets the Ambrosia bottle on the floor and approaches me, moving with predatory slowness. I'm frozen in place, my skin pebbling as she tuts in disapproval, like I'm a kid who got caught with her hand in the cookie jar.

"Oh, *sweetie*. You're making a mistake." Sasha shakes her head as she steps closer to me, hands stuffed in her pockets. Now she's close enough that I smell her breath. Mint and sulfur. "Believe me: You don't want to go out there."

All I can manage is a faint, "Yes, I do."

Her lips form a thin red line, the way my stepmother's did whenever she was disappointed. "Look at yourself, Crystal! You've lost so much weight. You've been entirely transformed!" Sasha points to the glass doors. The light filtering through is fainter than I remember it being, as if the sun is finally setting after an eternal day. "You leave, and all of that progress will be lost. Your hard work will have meant nothing."

I think of myself the day before I lost myself to Mount Olympus, standing in front of the bathroom mirror. My bloated belly. My puffed-up cheeks. As I ponder Sasha's warning, my resolve wavers.

Sidling closer to me, Sasha runs a sympathetic hand up and down my arm, making me shiver. "You could be happy here if you'd just let yourself be. You were happy, weren't you? Until you started to remember."

My hand instinctively clamps around my necklace as I try to keep Sasha from worming her way into my mind. My jaw tightens as I try to resist the pull of her words, but I keep glancing down at the bottle of Ambrosia she set on the floor.

As if on cue, Sasha reaches back and picks up the bottle. She taps the bottle with a manicured nail, and now I'm staring at it, watching the liquid slosh around in its plastic vessel. I bite my lip, balling up my fists, the cross pendant digging into my skin to the point of pain. It's no good, though. When she extends the bottle to me, I snatch it with my free hand.

My body quakes with the weight of indecision. I know what I want; my parched mouth, my aching shins, my feeble mind—they all are screaming at me to open the bottle and fall back into that state of blissful distraction that I've become so accustomed to. I let go of the necklace, my quivering hand hovering over the lid of the bottle.

"I really don't know why this is such a hard decision," Sasha says, propping herself on her desk and crossing her legs. "I mean, really. You've got no life to go back to. No one out there who gives a damn about your fat ass."

My eyes drop to the floor as the truth of her words cut me. I sift through the fragmented half-memories for anything to combat them, but honestly, I can't think of a single soul who would miss me. Ugly. Depressed. Boring. Dumb. *"Fat pig."*

No one's crying about my being gone. No one's blowing up my phone with concerned texts.

My fingers wrap around the lid. Wrenching off the cap, I drop it, and I hear it clatter against the floor.

And then I remember. A text message, the last one I read before coming here. From Dad: **Please call me, Crystal. I love you.**

I loosen my grip on the bottle. Something clicks in my mind: the fragmented memories start to come together.

Someone picks me up in strong arms, whirling me around while I scream with delight.

I careen downhill on a bike, fighting to keep myself steady while someone cheers me on.

Someone slips a silver necklace around my neck, whispers something in my ear, and holds me close.

A tear traces a path down my cheek. *Was it him all along?*

Try as I might, I still can't remember for sure; the fragments are all I have. Still...hope is hope—the same hope that made me stand on my weak legs and come to face Sasha in the first place makes my mind hum with possibilities.

Makes me tip over the Ambrosia bottle and dump it on the floor at Sasha's feet. It hisses as it pools between us like a nuclear waste spill.

And instantly, I'm overwhelmed by a sense of liberation. Seeing the Ambrosia spill is like seeing my own shackles fall to the floor. But without even looking up, I can feel Sasha's anger burning toward me.

When I do look up, I wish I hadn't. Her perfect appearance warps, her eyes flickering from a striking gray to a malevolent red. Her clean-cut visage collapses in on itself, that ever-present smile replaced with a grimace, revealing gritted teeth sharp enough to tear my throat out.

Her body shakes violently as if bearing the aftershocks of an explosion within itself. I take a few steps backward when she leans closer to me, raising her fists and unfurling them as if preparing to strangle me. Her hands glow red, fire engulfing her fingers and crawling up her forearms as reaches out to grab me.

My heart galloping wildly in my chest, I barely evade the demon's grasp as I make my way toward a shelf embedded in the desk. I hurl everything I can find at it: staplers, books, binders. But she keeps coming, undeterred by my assaults. Cupping her hands together, she grins wickedly as a ball of fire grows beneath her fingers.

She takes a step backward, poising herself to launch the fireball.

Reaching behind me, I grab a computer monitor and snatch it up.

Sasha launches a fireball the size of a basketball in my direction. Fueled by adrenaline, I leap out of the way and, at the same time, raise the computer monitor high and crack it over her head. Sasha stumbles backward, though the force isn't quite enough to topple her. Her face contorts in rage, and she charges me, her grotesque, inhuman shrieking echoing throughout the lobby. Tearing the monitor from the desktop it's attached to, I run, slipping out of the way just in time to avoid her attack. She skids to keep from slamming against the other end of the desk, and that's when I slam the screen against her skull one last time. This time, she crumples to the floor. The fire crawling up her arms gradually fades to a simmer.

She's still alive, still conscious. But I take advantage of her momentary weakness, scrambling over to her and slipping my hand into her front pocket.

Just as my fingers find the small keyring, Sasha rears up, now shifting into Valmath's form.

Sasha's painted face is replaced with his vicious frown, her petite frame by his sinewy body. A veil of flame forms a halo around his whole body, burning my forearm, but not before I manage to clamp my hand around the keys and wrestle it from beneath the khaki pocket.

Sliding backward, I cry out in agony as I stuff the keys into my pocket, next to the scissors.

Valmath is standing over me—towering over me like a flaming redwood as I use my weak, singed arms to crawl away from him. Heat radiates from his body, making me want to shield my face from him when he gets too close. I have to get up, but simply dropping to the floor is proving to be a perilous mistake; getting back up using these torn shins will be agonizing.

Behind me, I hear the electrical hum of the security screens—and I have an idea.

Valmath prepares a fireball twice the size of Sasha's and leans back, preparing to strike. Ignoring the torment in my shins, I crawl to my feet and scramble toward the open door to the back room. The heat of the demon's flames propel me forward, and within moments, I'm in the security room, slamming the door in Valmath's face.

I have the keys! I try to reassure myself as I search for something— anything—to barricade the door. *He can't get in without the keys!*

It's a laughably delusional thought, but I can't afford to despair now. I have an idea the only idea I have, so I'll have to make the most of it. I find a heavy filing cabinet and push it in front of the door, gritting my teeth and hissing as my limbs cry out in agony.

The door handle jiggles as if someone is trying to wrench it with his bare hands. A hysterical laugh explodes from my chest as I realize Valmath is, indeed, locked out.

For now.

The moment of relief doesn't last long, though. A body slams against the steel door, making the entire room tremble with the impact. Another slam, and hairline cracks extend from the door's hinges like spiderwebs.

The steel absorbs the heat from Valmath's flames.

I don't have long. Seconds, maybe.

My heart pounding along with the sound of Valmath attempting to down the door, I move toward the security screens and find the panel that Valmath had me touch—the device that captured my darkest memories.

"Half a soul..." I repeat Valmath's cryptic words as I reach forward to touch the panel again.

Out of the corner of my eye, I see fiery red light blossoming in the center of the door.

"I hope I'm right..."

I place a trembling hand on the panel.

Chapter 21

Nothing happens at first. While the sound of Valmath's banging on the door echoes menacingly throughout the room, I close my eyes, focusing only on the feeling of the dark panel beneath my palm—waiting to feel something, anything.

At last, I feel it. A sensation like static electricity courses throughout my hand, surging up my arm. It's painful, but I keep my hand pressed against the panel, shifting my gaze to the flickering screens. As the shocking sensation dies down, one by one, the screens change, fading to black at first and then lighting up again, showing scenes from my life.

My life.

Immediately, my eyes are drawn to the center of the screen, to that scene between Jace and me, when he stormed out of my life for the last time. The moment before everything spiraled out of control.

I force myself to look at the other screens, and I notice a grim pattern: They all depict negative moments in my life. Schoolyard bullying. Screaming matches between me and my parents. Jace's abuse. The customers who'd mocked me at Hungry Harry's. Any moment in my life that had made me feel worse about myself is on full display, playing in a vicious loop over and over.

Thud! I whirl around in time to see one of the door hinges come flying off the wall. Valmath is getting into the room. And I have no idea what to do once he does.

My eyes dart from screen to screen, searching for some clue, some chink in Valmath's extravagant illusion. That's when I see it: one screen, in the upper right-hand corner, shows fragmented clips no longer than 3 to 4 seconds in length. The clips are completely soundless, and when they fade away, the screen fades to static before the next one begins.

I recognize these scenes, though.

Strong arms. Bicycle. Necklace.

Dad?

Thud! Thud! The steel door is about to crumble beneath the weight of Valmath's fiery body.

I focus on that one screen, feeling the panel growing warm beneath my palm. I will the memories Valmath stole from me to return. I will my half soul to fly into my body.

Another hinge comes flying off the door. Valmath's inhuman roar makes all the air in the room go cold.

I need to do something! I clamber atop the desk beneath the security screens and reach out to touch the screen broadcasting the fragmented memories.

When I do, my hand sinks into the screen, similarly to how the glass had melted beneath me during my encounter with Clarissa. It's like I've dipped my hand into a pool of warm water, and I'm so stunned that I jolt backward, falling off the desk. Steadying myself with my free hand, I reach as far into the screen as I can, watching as Valmath pounds his way into the room.

Something is happening.

The further I reach into the screen-pool, the warmer the water feels. I feel a sensation like heat pulsing, sinking into my skin. I stretch my fingers out as far as they'll go, grasping at whatever light is emitting this pleasant warmth.

There's a crash and a scream of crumbling metal. Valmath, still encircled by wicked flames, stalks into the security room. When he sees me reaching into the screen, the cocky smirk on his face disappears and is replaced by a worried expression.

I reach further into the screen, standing on tiptoe and feeling my arm muscles strain with effort.

The warmth in the water intensifies, and out of the corner of my eye, I see light explode beneath the screen. I turn to face it, but I quickly have to turn away; the brightness is too much to handle, a blinding explosion of brilliant pain that takes my breath away.

Valmath sees what's happening, and his eyes burn like twin fires boring into me. He charges me. I try to dodge him without taking my arm out of the screen, but he knocks me to the ground, briefly setting my leggings on fire and burning my calves in the process.

But he's too late. I topple to the floor, cracking my head against the edge of the desk and rolling around to douse the flames on my pants. I scream in pain—but not in fear. Instead, I'm struck with a strange sensation of lightness, like that of a wind rushing into me and threatening to lift me ten feet off the ground. That same warmth from the screen now rests in the center of my chest, blossoming and pulsing through every vein.

My soul. Tears spill over as I realize for the first time in ages, I feel whole. Complete.

Human.

Seeing my reaction, Valmath roars, angry flames spewing from his mouth and charring the ceiling. I stumble to my feet and leap over the ruined door, making my way back into the lobby. And despite my pain, I'm smiling.

Because the memories are back. All of them.

Dad picks me up in his strong arms, whirling me around while I scream with delight.

I careen downhill on a bike, fighting to keep myself steady while Dad cheers me on.

Dad slips a silver necklace around my neck, whispers a prayer in my ear, and holds me close. Peaceful strength swells within me, and I sleep.

Dad calls for the first time in four years, and I ignore him.

I have to get back.

I make a beeline for the lobby doors, my breath coming out in terrified wheezes as Valmath chases after me. My fingers wrap around the metal door handle and pull but to no avail. Locked?

Valmath is coming closer. A cinder flies off his burning body and lands on my shirt before dying out. My overspent muscles scream with the effort of trying to wrench the door open, but it won't budge.

"No, no, no, no!" My breaths come out too fast, and my heart rattles against my chest like a caged animal as a blistering heat at my back announces the demon's steady approach. I groan in agony, tears streaming down my face.

In the end, when my skin boils with blisters, I give up. There has to be another way out. Not daring to turn around and face Valmath, I run toward the other end of the room and try to run out of the lobby. But with a flick of his wrist, he summons a wall of fire rush to block my path. I skid to a halt just in time to avoid careening face-first into the flames.

I try the other direction, and another wall of fire shoots up.

Within seconds, I'm entirely encircled in flames. The heat makes me feel weak; I want to shield my eyes, but I don't dare take my eyes off the demon.

Now that I'm trapped, Valmath stalks toward me, his imposing form shrinking marginally as he does. The halo of fire enveloping his body dies down, and he's smiling that brash, boyish smile of his. I back up, fear squeezing my racing heart like a vice, until I feel the heat from the ring of fire warning me to go no further.

I stand there, chest heaving, jaw tight, fire lighting up my already blistering back—knowing the end is near.

The demon shakes his head, a low laugh rumbling in his chest. "I don't want to kill you, Crystal."

I'm confused at first, but then I remember. *My soul.*

I have something he wants.

"N-no..." It's all I can say. The heat is too much, and there's no escape from it.

Valmath stops moving toward me. He shuts his eyes, raising his hands as if to launch fire at me. Despite his telling me he doesn't intend to kill me, I instinctively flinch, falling to the ground and curling in a protective ball.

There's a rip of electricity, and I try to roll out of the way to avoid the assault. I'm too late, though; the shock emanates from my head and courses throughout my entire body. My heart beats unnaturally fast, and I worry that it will explode under the intense rush of painful pressure.

I wait for the inevitable darkness—to finally blink out of existence after fighting so hard for my freedom.

Instead, the opposite happens. The lightning-bolt sensation kicks my mind into overdrive, and I swear I can feel Valmath's demonic fingers rifling through my darkest thoughts until he finds exactly what he's looking for.

Don't look, don't look, I tell myself when I feel a familiar presence appear before me. Every hair on my skin stands on end. My still-racing heart drops into my stomach. Even above the oppressive smell of smoke, I can smell his cologne. I want to cry and scream and curse all at once because he's here. I know he's here.

"Crys," Jace says. His voice is distorted, watery. But it's his, all right, and hearing it after all this time fills me with unease, making me feel as though my skin is crawling with spiders.

Shock forces my eyes open. Looking up, I see him standing before me, a shadowy silhouette against the wall of fire. Thankfully, he's whole, not covered in blood and gore like in my hallucination. But he's giving me that awful look, the one where his eyes are big and soft with mock concern, but his brow is furrowed in frustration. That look that says, *I cared about you once, but now you disgust me. Now, you're not worth my time. Not worth my love.*

"Jace?" The word comes out in a barely audible whimper.

He just stands there.

"Why are you here?" I ask.

He shifts forward slightly, and his face twists up in scorn, his brown eyes probing me. "Damn, Crystal. You've really let yourself go."

It doesn't make any sense. I've been working out incessantly, I've lost so much weight, and he *still* thinks I'm too fat. It's been a year since I've seen him alive, at least, and that tone of disapproval stings just as much as it did before.

He sucks his teeth contemptuously. "I mean, it's like you don't even try."

I shut my eyes and turn my back to the apparition. "Not real, not real, not real." But listening to his criticism makes me feel as though I've been knocked back in time. Not only the words themselves but the distinctive rise and fall of his tenor are direct echoes of so many bad conversations we had before everything finally fell apart.

The sickly-sweet smell of his sweat and cologne overpower my senses. I can feel the heat of his body and his breath on my face, and I know if I open my eyes, he's going to be right there in front of me.

"The hell do you mean, 'not real'?" I can hear the arrogant smile in his voice. When I don't respond, he mutters, "Crazy bitch."

It's all too much. A heady mixture of hatred and fear churns within me. I take one look at that smug face and shove him out of the way. I take a few steps away from him, but can only manage a few feet before hitting a wall of fire.

My hands curl into fists. I'm getting real tired of being trapped.

"You're a mess, Crys." Before I can react, he's at my side once again. He cups my face in his hands and tilts my chin upward. I want to yank free, but I'm too close to the flames. "Why can't you just...stop being so *sensitive* all the time? You take everything so damn seriously."

I tense up at his touch, shrugging away from him, my arms crossed over my chest. I will myself to be strong against him, but my head feels funny, like the past is snaking its way into my mind, waking up sleeping neurons and forcing me to reenact old conflicts.

I bristle and take a half step backward, shrugging out of his grip. I can sense the feeling of déjà vu, but I say it anyway: "Why do you have to be such a dick?"

He seems unmoved by my insult. "Yeah, well," he begins, shrugging his shoulders. "Maybe if you weren't such a fat pig, I'd be more attracted to you."

And there it is again. The pain, the shame, the bewilderment from that night a year ago. Over the past year, I've let these words take up way too much space in my mind, but there's something about hearing them—physically hearing them from Jace's own voice—that adds to the sting. I stare at his stony, unrepentant face, barely holding my ground as I'm rocked by a tidal wave of trauma. The door slams. The phone rings. "We regret to inform you... " Jace, covered in blood. Jace in a coffin. *My fault.*

"And..." He steps uncomfortably close, leaning his head in so that he's able to whisper right in my ear.

My hair stands on end. *What do you mean "and"?* I've replayed this scene from my past over and over again in my mind, and there had never been an "and" before.

He takes his time finishing the sentence, relishing my state of suspense. "You know what else? If it weren't for your sorry excuse for a body, our baby would still be alive."

At that moment, I'm stunned, feeling as though my spirit has just been kicked out of my of my body. Ice crawls through my veins despite the wall of fire because he *said* it. He actually said it.

Sure, he'd danced around it before. He'd made slick comments here and there, had muttered things under his breath. But to say outright that I was to blame for our baby's death? No, that wasn't his style. But through manipulation and snideness and passive-aggression, he made his message clear: My body wasn't just fat; it was revolting, despicable, and it caused us to lose the one bright spot in our miserable relationship.

Jace backs up, and I'm finally able to breathe freely. He looks at me, shining eyes daring me to respond. Arms crossed in arrogant defiance. He raises his eyebrows. "Well?"

A tear slides down my cheek. "Well, what?" I ball up my fists as I try to keep from breaking down completely. "What do you expect me to say?"

He doesn't answer, remains still, and glares at me. Waiting.

Strangely enough, Jace's unexpected insult gives me a sense of freedom.

If he can change the year-old narrative to his advantage, so can I.

I can say what I've been wanting to say at last.

"There's no point in arguing with you," I say. "There's no point in apologizing." I shrug and gesture to him. "You're not even real. But even if you were, you'd be well past the point of reasoning."

Jace rolls his eyes. "Right."

"We were a toxic match, you and me." I look at my feet, feeling my cheeks glow with shame. "I tried to deny it for so long. I didn't want my parents to be right...and sometimes..." My eyes sting with tears. "Sometimes you were so sweet. I mean, I didn't fall in love with a monster. You just...changed. You became one."

"Ha!" He steps toward me, and I force myself to stand my ground, even though every ounce of my being wants to turn and run. "Damn right, I changed. Being stuck with trash like you does things to a guy."

He grimaces. "If I became a 'monster,' it's because you made me one—your disgusting body and your piss-poor attitude."

And suddenly, I feel my strength beginning to waver as he hurls back the same words I've heard echo in the dark chasms of my own mind for the past year. *My fault, my fault...*

No.

Not my fault.

The realization doesn't hit me all at once like a sudden burst of strength. Rather, it's like ever since I decided to quit Ambrosia, there's been a steady drip of truth filling up the empty places within me, and I finally have the strength I need to accept reality.

It's not my fault Jace cheated on me.

It's not my fault he drove recklessly.

It's not my fault he died.

The baby...that's not my fault either.

All my life, I've been the type of person who has to be in control. The only way I've had to make sense of the chaos in my life is to blame myself for everything. Blame myself and fill my life with whatever distractions I can get my hands on when the guilt becomes too much to handle.

I look up at Jace. The flames dance in his dark eyes, which bore into me with pure hatred. I stare back at him, my jaw firmly set.

"Well?" He makes the mistake of stepping backward, giving me enough room to back away from the flames. "You gonna just stand here like an idiot or what?"

I want to slap him, but I hold myself back when another idea hits me—hopefully, a better one. Turning my back to him, I cross my arms and steadily move toward the other end of the flame circle, facing the desk.

Facing the registration contracts.

I hear him coming up behind me, and I conjure up all the whiny self-pity I can manage. "Go away!" I shout.

He appears in front of me, just like I had hoped he would, towering over me. "What, you're just gonna pretend nothing ever happened?"

"Leave me alone!" I manage a few tears and let them fall down my cheek.

Jace scoffs. "Pitiful. You're actually crying? After all you've done to me, you don't get to cry."

Wait, I think. *Wait for the right moment.*

All of a sudden, Jace is holding a bottle of Ambrosia, as if he pulled it out of thin air. The bottle glows brightly, a gentle light compared to the harsh flames roaring in front of me, blocking me from freedom.

Once again, I can't tear my eyes from the Ambrosia. My heart jumps. My mouth waters.

Jace steps in close, suddenly gentle, tucking a strand of hair behind my ear like he used to, a gesture that always used to give me chills. This time, I don't pull away. Can't stop my body from trembling.

"You don't have to fight so hard, Crys." Jace's voice is soft and heavy. "You know what you want." He slides the plastic bottle into my shaking hands. The bottle is warm against my skin, and the strange light it emits makes my head feel hazy. "Here, nothing is holding you back from being who you want to be."

Who I want to be? My eyes snap up and glare at him.

This is the moment, I realize. My chest tightens, and my gaze snaps to Jace's smug face. My hands tighten around the Ambrosia bottle, and with one sudden motion, I lean back and knock Jace in the right temple with the heavy bottle.

I'm surprised by my own strength; Jace nearly crumbles under the blow, tilting to one side and covering his head with his hand as he cries out in pain.

I back up, still holding my weapon and preparing to strike back. "No. I'm *done*!"

Done letting you take up space in my mind.

He grits his teeth and prepares to retaliate, but before he can manage, I do what I've always dreamed about doing but never had the strength to do before. I raise the bottle high and aim for the groin.

Crying out, he stumbles backward and folds in on himself from the blow. I use the opportunity and shove him into the wall of fire. Jace's body absorbs the flames, and I leap over him and run like hell toward the reception desk, the keychain rattling in my pocket.

I can hardly contain my pride and joy from overcoming my ex's hold on me, but I know there's no time to celebrate. I've got to get out of here, and I know there's only one way.

Chapter 22

Hoisting myself over Sasha's desk, I fish the keyring out of my pocket and bolt toward the locked drawer. Only a few feet away, I hear Jace's pained cries morph into the sound of Valmath's enraged, demonic roar. Fingers trembling, I drop the keys and quickly recover them, trying one key after another, after another until the drawer finally slides open, revealing the folders marked with several names. *I did it!*

My skin prickles with goosebumps when I feel a presence behind me. Snatching back the key and pocketing it, I whirl around to face Jace, who is hunched over and has his fists balled up as if to strike. His body morphs grotesquely, Sasha's and Valmath's forms flickering in and out like some glitchy video game character.

I reach into the drawer to retrieve the files, but Valmath's form takes over.

I jump to my feet and run, my aching legs pumping beneath me. When I attempt to jump back over the desk, fiery hands seize my ankles, sending me crashing onto the floor. My chin slams against the desk, making my teeth knock together.

The demon draws me back to him. I kick and thrash to escape, but I'm locked in his vice-like grip. I feel blistering pain blossom beneath his hold. Screaming, I bolt upright and see that his hands are on fire again.

I continue to fight him, but he's too strong. My body twists and flails in the demon's grip, helpless, like a water-starved fish flopping in the sand.

Desperate, I reach under my shirt and pull my cross necklace over my head. Holding it by the chain, I straighten up and extend my arm outward, waving the pendant directly in front of Valmath's face.

At first, nothing changes. Valmath notices the object for a brief second but doesn't comment or attempt to move it away. Then, I notice him shift uncomfortably, subtly leaning away from the pendant.

Valmath releases his fiery hands from my ankles and prepares to ensnare my wrists.

And that's when I realize my plan is working.

When he's directly over me, I transfer the cross from one hand to another and slam it against his forehead just before he has time to grab me again.

He tries to pretend that he's not fazed by my assault, but the pain is evident in his expression. He grits his teeth and sews his eyes shut, even as he laughs. "Clearly, you've watched too many horror movies."

I'm not buying his bravado. Instead, I'm noticing how his limbs quiver beneath his weight and how his skin is growing pale. I send up a silent, frantic prayer, mustering as much calm strength as I can before I skitter out from underneath him. Once I'm free, I hold the cross with one hand and use the other to push him a few inches away from me. It's all I can manage, but it's enough.

Heart slamming in my chest, I force myself to stand. Force myself to run, to ignore the screaming pain encircling my ankles and stabbing through my shins. Valmath is up within seconds, charging after me like a savage bull.

I rush toward the open desk drawer.

Before I can reach it, Valmath ensnares my arms with his fiery hands, slamming me against the door to Sasha's back office. He tightens his grip, and I scream as my skin boils in his grasp.

A sadistic smile climbs up his face, and he begins to lift me high off the ground. Panic grips me as I continue to feel myself slide higher, Valmath's body growing taller every second as the burning pain spreads all throughout my arms. My feet kick wildly, trying to catch him in the chest, in the groin, anywhere.

But instead, I hit something metal, and pain shoots up my calf. *The doorknob!*

Pain makes tears flow freely, but eventually, my foot finds the door handle again and presses down hard. The door flies open, and I'm airborne for a moment as Valmath drops me, stunned by the sudden movement of the door. Our bodies spill into the security room. His grows to its original size as he recovers from the sudden movement, and I dash past him, out of the security room and back toward the open drawer.

"Come on...come on..." I crouch on the floor and flick through the files until I find my name. Snapping up the folder, I back up against the desk, tucking the file into my waistband under my shirt, and I feel something metal knock against the wood. The scissors! Valmath stands up in the back room, preparing for another assault, and I prepare myself.

"Give me that contract," Valmath growls.

He lumbers back into the lobby and is in front of me within moments, eyes wild with fury and sharp teeth bared. My cross is stored in my front pocket, and the folder and the scissors are behind my back. I drop the folder on the floor and step on it, and just as he notices what I've done, I use the scissors to stab him hard in the leg, where the knee meets the thigh. He lets loose a wild roar and stumbles backward, still standing. A river of thick black blood trickles down his leg.

I back up, sliding the folder backward and never removing my weight from it. Valmath makes a move to snatch the scissors from me, but he's too slow. I catch him in the hand.

The fire in his hands is spreading up his arms, heading toward his chest. *Good.*

He reaches out to snatch me again, and I duck down, tucking my head under my hands and stabbing him in his calf once I'm low enough. He backs up several feet as the blood flows, and the fiery flame is now spreading from his chest to his head and throughout his body.

So when he finally knocks me to the ground, I hold up my file folder to shield myself from the flames. The contract I'd signed—the contract that had bound me to Mount Olympus all this time—crumples before my eyes. When the fire spreads to the edge of the folder, I release it, my fingertips singed by the flames. It careens toward my face, and I yank my head out of the way just in time to avoid it.

Seeing the ruined file folder, Valmath puts out the flames enveloping his body, but it's too late. Nothing happens.

I don't know what I expected to feel. Is this all it would take to get home?

Was this whole plan just a waste of time?

Valmath rears up, a low growl escaping from his throat.

Cringing at the murderous look in his eyes, I sit up and try to crawl out from underneath him.

His hand flies back and strikes my cheek so hard that I hit the floor again. I grit my teeth as my head bounces hard against the floor.

There's a shift in the air, a sudden wind, barely noticeable but enough to make the hairs on my arm stand on end.

Valmath's eyes turn into slits like knife-blades. He suddenly stands, and his eyes widen in confusion when he stares down at me. "You *bitch!*"

My joints stiff, I struggle to slide away from him and toward the contract drawer.

The cold wind picks up, blowing through my knotted ponytail. Not only that, but when I look around the lobby, I notice that the walls are fading away gradually; it's as though I'm stuck between two transitioning frames of a film. Even Valmath, stomping across the floor and reigniting the flames in his hands, appears semitransparent against a backdrop of a dusky landscape.

Hoisting myself back behind the circular desk, I hear something sizzle through the air. I duck in time to avoid the fiery blasts he's aiming at me. I feel the warmth against my face as they slam into the concrete wall.

I scramble toward the open filing cabinet where I'd found my soul-binding contract. I pick up as many similar documents as I can find and bundle them in my arms; I double-check to make sure I retrieve the ones marked "WAKE, GIDEON" and "WAKE, ELIJAH."

The wind is picking up, making my teeth chatter. Mount Olympus is fading away faster by the second.

"Hey, asshole!" I say, popping up from behind the desk, and I hope he can't tell how worried I am that this won't work. "I'm leaving!"

Valmath's eyes become slits again, and his chest heaves rapidly as if he's hyperventilating from anger. His hands form a fireball.

"So I must be the only person to have ever figured out how to escape your little trap, aren't I?" I manage a cool, confident smile, but my mind is screaming, *I don't have time, I don't have time!*

Valmath, seeing the contracts in my hand, kills the fireball, not wanting to make the same mistake twice. Instead, he rushes toward me, arms outstretched and ready to tear me limb from limb. I leap over the desk from the other side and make my way toward the still-burning ring of fire.

Slamming into me, Valmath sends me sprawling toward the floor, face-down, only inches away from the flames. I feel the contracts pinned beneath me as I struggle against his weight. It's useless, though. He's too strong.

It's then that I notice something strange: the ground feels colder beneath me, like bare concrete. A couple of dead leaves tumble toward me, brushing against my cheek. I hear a distant chirping sound, like a cricket.

"No!" I hear Valmath's voice from above me; he notices something happening too. In his moment of surprise, he lifts himself just enough to allow me to escape. He quickly recovers me, catching me by the wrists and shouting, "You won't leave here alive!"

But not before I shove the contracts into the ring of fire.

Chapter 23

The contracts burn, consumed by the wall of flames, folding in on themselves before transforming into ash. The heat emanating from the fire feels like it's enough to make my skin melt away, but I can't tear my eyes away from the beautiful sight of those documents' destruction.

Valmath still has me pinned down, but he, too, watches the documents burn. His gaze is distant, his expression, crestfallen. When he slides off of me, I almost think that he'll be too depressed to take any further action against me.

I'm not so lucky.

When Valmath stands, I scoot myself away from the fire ring, and he stalks toward me, forming another fireball in his hands. I reach up to hoist myself back over the desk, but the pain in my legs slows me down.

The fireball is bigger than a basketball when he hurls it at me, and I try to duck behind the desk, but I know I won't make it in time.

Two thoughts occur almost simultaneously as the flames sail toward me: One, *I'm going to die.* Two, *Why does Valmath look...transparent?*

When the fireball approaches, I wince, too tired and weak to avoid it. Somehow, though, it passes through me, unfelt and barely visible. I crash-land behind the desk, my heart racing from the near-death experience and my mind unable to accept what had just happened.

And then I realize it. *It's working!*

I pop up from behind the desk, watching as Valmath approaches, his mouth opening and closing in a stream of furious words. No sound comes out, though. Everything seems to fade from around me—the desk, the ring of fire, Valmath. There's a pulsing sensation in my head, like a heavy weight sliding into place, and all at once, the translucent images vanish. I'm alone in the dark, in the cold.

When the pulsing in my head ceases, I examine my surroundings—a decrepit, abandoned concrete building. Dead leaves, blown in through the building's busted windows, skitter along the floor and gather in piles.

For a brief moment, I panic, unsure of where I am, but my panic quickly turns to relief when I realize that it doesn't matter.

Because I'm not in Mount Olympus anymore.

Because I'm free.

Exhausted, emotionally and physically, I collapse. Black spots dance along the edges of my vision as my chest labors to haul in the crisp night air.

A tear slips down my cheek.

I did it. I got out.

And after what seemed like an eternity of constant movement, all I want to do is sleep. I close my eyes, letting the darkness take me.

* * *

The first thing I notice when I come to is the cold—the pure, bitter cold of the approaching winter. The kind that makes summer skin crack and bleed, not the damp cold that I had grown used to in the bowels of Mount Olympus.

I wake up with a start, my body shooting upward with such force that I give myself whiplash. Bleary-eyed and aching from the rude awakening, I look around. I remember.

There's something familiar about the abandoned building. Something very similar to Mount Olympus. Sasha's huge circular desk is gone, as is the linoleum floor and the overall polished look of the lobby. But there's a door where the door to the security room should be and one that should lead to the weight room. A flutter of worry makes my heart race as I consider the idea that I didn't make it home after all, that maybe this is just another one of Valmath's "redecoration" projects.

With some effort, I stand and am relieved to find that my injuries are gone. The shin splints, burn marks, and other injuries I'd acquired through both overtraining and in the fight with Valmath and his associates are nothing but a memory. I sigh, feeling my knotted-up chest relax for the first time in what seems like forever.

But once I've found my footing, I notice a familiar enemy.

My gut has returned. The body I worked so hard to sculpt in Mount Olympus is gone, just like the demon warned me it would be. For a moment, I wonder if this whole ordeal has been nothing but a dream. I wish I could really believe that.

I run my hands over my rolls, the ones I've spent so much time despising. The desire to lose weight hasn't gone away, but it is mixed with another feeling—the comfort of finally being back in my own skin. Of finally feeling whole.

I look down at myself and smile. Despite being heavy as ever, I've never felt lighter.

Shivering from the cold, I step toward the door to where the security room should be, wondering if I'll see security cameras behind it. Instead, soft morning light filters through a window. Peering out the window, I gaze across a vast grassy field. There are no roads nor any sign of civilization as far as the eye can see, and I wonder what possessed me to drive this far in the first place.

But when the sunlight hits me through the broken glass, I know.

I'm home.

Tears brim in my eyes. I can't believe I did it.

Turning away from the window, I step on something hard, and there's a sound like plastic crunching beneath my foot. Looking down, I move my foot to see a flip phone on the ground. I pick it up and open it, but its screen is black.

That's when I notice the collection of cell phones scattered around the "security room." They lie on the ground and on rusted metal shelves that protrude from the wall. Hope explodes in my chest, and I rifle through them to find my phone.

After a moment's searching, I find it: the smartphone in the black and yellow case lies in the corner of one of the shelves. Its screen is black, but I press and hold the "on" button and tap my foot impatiently as I wait for the screen to come to life.

I hear the shuffle of feet against the concrete and whirl around, terrified that Valmath has followed me back into my world. Instead, a young man in a disheveled business suit leans in the door frame, his glasses magnifying his bewildered eyes. A taller man with an eagle tattoo comes up behind him, looking around like he's landed on a different planet.

Setting the phone down, I cover my face with my hands, open-mouthed and crying tears of joy. *It worked!*

At length, Gideon smiles, and the confusion falls from his face. "Crystal."

I move my hands from my face, smiling. "You found him."

Gideon wipes a tear from his eyes.

Elijah smiles at him. "Yeah."

Out of the corner of my eye, I see a flash of light. I look at the shelf where I laid my phone, and I snatch it up when I see it's come to life.

"Your phones are probably in here," I tell Gideon and Elijah without looking at them.

My eyes lock on the screen, as if the harder I stare at it, the quicker I can make the phone find a signal. Time passes, though, and nothing happens. No notifications light up my screen, and my confidence melts. "*No one cares about your fat ass.*"

I push aside Sasha's words as I pocket the phone. All throughout the abandoned building, I hear voices, see people who had been trapped within Mount Olympus slowly drifting back into reality. The boy I'd seen trying to detox from Ambrosia bursts through the lobby doors, laughing like a maniac. The old man who'd tried killing himself to escape weeps uncontrollably and says, "Thank you, Jesus!" over and over again until he disappears through the front doors.

I'm about to make my way out when I hear a voice behind me curse.

Turning around, I see Gideon holding his phone like he's about to crush it.

He shouts, "Two months? I've been here two months!"

In my haste to check for messages, I hadn't even bothered to check the date on my phone.

Gideon came here after I did...

I swipe the phone open, and my heart hits the floor.

Five months.

I think about my family, my job, and everyone I've ever bothered to have in my life. To them, I might as well be dead.

Elijah emerges from the room and joins his brother. Gideon wipes tears away from his eyes. Elijah looks pale, blank, and I realize he must have been trapped in Mount Olympus just as long as I was. If not longer. I approach them.

"How...?" Elijah can't bring himself to finish the sentence.

"It's been so long." Gideon can't stop looking at his phone. "So many people... They thought..." His lip quivers, and he turns his head before breaking into tears.

How do we bring ourselves back from the dead?

I muster up as much courage as I have left within me and smile at the brothers. "It'll be okay," I tell them.

The words seem hollow, though. "Okay" doesn't seem to apply to a future riddled with such uncertainty. I do know one thing, though: Anything is better than the alternative.

* * *

We exit the lobby doors, wading through the sea of tall grass toward the abandoned cars in front of the concrete building. All the while, ex-prisoners of Mount Olympus make their way toward their cars, crying, laughing, or simply walking in reverent silence as we do.

It's not as crowded as I remember. My heart goes cold, and I try not to consider the possibility that there are still people trapped in Valmath's illusion.

I catch sight of a figure crossing the grass toward us. As soon as I'm able to register who it is, my heart lightens up all over again. As he draws closer, I can smell the cigarette smoke wafting off his clothes.

The old man shuffles across the field, a look of bewilderment twisting up his already wrinkled face. When he finally, makes eye contact with me, he stops in his tracks, and the confusion in his expression quickly turns to terror. He points a shaking finger at me. "Y-you...?"

I want to wrap him up in a huge hug and thank him for saving my life, even though he doesn't even realize it. But I don't want to give the poor man a heart attack. To him, he might as well be looking at a ghost.

But I can't stop myself from smiling and extending my hand toward him. He stares at it for a while. Then, when finally convinced that I'm not a malevolent phantom, he lets me shake it. Opening up my phone case, I pull out a few ten-dollar bills—the only cash I have—and hand them to him.

"Thank you," I say. "You helped me find my way home."

* * *

Gideon's car is near the front of the "parking lot," half-concealed by tall grass, and Elijah's isn't far from it. I stop and let him wrap me up in an embrace.

"Thank you," Gideon says. "I remember...how you tried to help me."

I grin. "I remember how you tried to kill me. But no hard feelings."

He smiles. "Take care of yourself."

We separate, and Elijah shakes my hand. "I hope we meet again someday," he says.

I nod. "I'd like that."

There's a moment of silence, save for the sound of birds crying overhead. It pains me to leave behind these familiar faces of people who have been through Hell—or *almost* Hell—with me together, but I take a step backward, and then leave them behind.

I stuff my hands in my pockets and scan the tall grass for my car, praying that the brothers will be okay.

That we'll all be okay.

* * *

"Come *on*..." I twist the ignition key again, only to hear sputtering. "Don't do this to me."

The field outside Mount Olympus is in a state of chaos. Several people are fighting to get their cars to start, some are working together over jumper cables, and others wander around the field with their phones held high, trying to get reception. Some abandon their vehicles and walk or carpool.

"Come on," I demand through gritted teeth. But the engine within my old beater won't respond to my efforts. "Come on!" I slam the steering wheel with my fists.

What now?

As if on cue, a bright red pickup truck glides up next to me. Its window rolls down, and a head of platinum blonde hair pops out.

"Need a ride?" Sadie asks.

* * *

We ride in silence for several minutes, save for the classic country music floating from Sadie's speakers. The desire to make conversation eludes me as I stare at my phone, waiting for cell service.

What if no one bothered contacting me all this time?

The longer I stare at the useless phone screen, the more my frustration mounts. I sigh and put it under my thigh.

"Hey," Sadie says, her voice wavering. "I've been meaning to say... just, thanks for listening to me that time. About Lydia."

"Of course." It takes a moment to recall the conversation. "Did she ever call you?"

Sadie's smile lights up her whole face, and a few tears stream down her cheek. "Several times. She was worried. I guess...she really does care."

"That's fantastic." I smile, but my heart aches with jealousy.

To distract myself from the waiting, I peer out the window, even though there's not much worth looking at. Farmhouses. Soybean fields. Abandoned buildings. The monochromatic landscape seems to blend together in a way that's almost hypnotic. My eyes grow heavy, and I rest my head against the window.

When my phone finally does vibrate, it feels like a lightning strike. I bolt upright and snatch it up with clammy hands.

My phone vibrates with a succession of notifications.

Thirty-four voicemails. 164 missed texts. Most of them are from Dad, but there are even a few from Mom. From work. From Cici. From loved ones I'd forgotten I even had while I was trapped in Mount Olympus. My eyes water as I scroll through the messages and watch their tones shift from worried to terrified to sorrowful and then hopeless.

Dad's most recent text says, **I wish I'd done things right the first time. Now it's too late.**

I can't help but laugh, even as tears blind my vision. I can't help but think that it's I who didn't "do things right." I was so blinded by hurt that I ended up losing myself entirely. I almost surrendered my entire world, not knowing how important it was to me, even in its turmoil.

I see Sadie grin out of the corner of my eye. "Feels good, doesn't it?"

I nod, suppressing the urge to sob. "Feels real good."

* * *

Sadie drops me off at my crappy apartment complex. The place never felt like home before, but now, the idea of crawling under the covers of my own bed makes me feel warm all over. Once my feet hit the pavement, and Sadie and I exchange our goodbyes and well wishes, it's all I can do to keep from running up the flimsy staircase leading to my second-story apartment.

Once I reach the front door, my spirit sinks all over again.

It's been five months.

I try the lock anyway. My key doesn't work, no matter how hard I try. Five months. I yank the useless key out of the doorknob. Of course they changed the locks.

I turn to signal for Sadie, but her little red truck has already peeled out into the street.

I grip my cross necklace, squeezing it tightly. "What now?"

* * *

Sitting at the base of an oak tree outside my apartment, I hold my phone. My leg bounces as I try to work up the willpower to press "dial" for the first time in ages.

I'm homeless. Penniless. Legally dead. I know who to call for help, but I can't bring myself to do it.

"It's been so long," I whisper.

Too long.

I've been isolated too long. For far, far too long, I've let my own fears and mistakes drive away any chance at a new start. The press of a button could wipe that all away, but once again, fear makes me hesitate.

No, I coach myself. Not anymore.

I swipe open my phone, and my fingertips hover over the contact list. *What will he say?*

My lip quivers as I beat back the voices in my head that tell me not to trust him. Not to try again. That I can't handle any more rejection than I've already faced.

But I close my eyes and breathe deeply, summoning up courage from my newly restored soul.

There once was a man who told me I was worthless. His words shredded at my spirit—had weakened me. And when he finally died, I bottled up his ghost and let it whisper in my ear, poisoning me from beyond the grave.

But in the dark halls of Mount Olympus, I released him. Despite my insecurities and my baggage, I was strong enough to exorcise him.

And in light of that, I decide I'm strong enough to do a whole lot more.

I press the call button. He picks up after two rings.

"Crystal?" The cracked, fragile voice on the other end hardly sounds like him. "I–is that you?"

"Hey, Dad." Tears freely flow, but I don't bother to wipe them away. "You're alive!"

I cover my mouth to hold back a threatening sob. "Yeah. I'm okay, but I need some help. Do you think you could...?"

I can almost hear the strength rush into his tearful voice. "Anything. But where... Where did you go, Crystal?"

"It's hard to explain. I've— Well, we've got a lot to talk about."

I rest my head on the base of the tree, drinking in the sunshine filtering through the canopy of leaves hanging over me. Relishing the smell of earth mixed with exhaust fumes from passing cars.

Feeling my chest relax as the last cords of resentment snap away from my heart.

Feeling free at last.

When Dad and I hang up after making arrangements for him to pick me up, I lie in the grass and smile. I rest my hands on the stomach that I've loathed for so long.

Tomorrow, I may look in the mirror and want to make a change. But this time, it'll be different. I'll no longer be a slave to the voices of the past. At last, I can combat the echo of *"fat pig"* with the truths I've discovered.

I am strong.

I am human.

I am loved.

Acknowledgments

To me, writing is more than a hobby or even a career—it's a journey. As I reflect on the time and effort that went into bringing *Ambrosia* to life, I can't help but think of the many people who have helped me throughout my journey to my first published novel.

My parents, Danny and Kim Campbell, were the first people to recognize my potential as a writer, and I'm so grateful to them for nurturing my interest in storytelling. I have fond childhood memories of bringing my short stories to my dad for feedback. My mom encouraged me by customizing my homeschool curriculum around my interest in writing. Looking back, I'm incredibly blessed that I had what I needed as a young writer: people who validated my dreams and pointed me to opportunities to improve.

My sisters, Hannah and Phoebe, and my brother, Daniel, were crucial to my development as a writer as well. The time we spent playing out imaginary scenarios and writing stories and comics together strengthened my love of writing. My siblings still support and believe in me, and for that, I am incredibly grateful. Daniel—an aspiring novelist and screenwriter himself—has been especially helpful throughout the publication process. I look forward to his regular phone calls about all things writing, and I can't wait to see his stories hit bookstores too!

My husband, Dale, has been my biggest fan throughout our fifteen-year relationship. He has seen me when I've felt most insecure about my writing, and he's been a comforting presence during those times. When I'm tough on myself, he balances me out, seeing the good in even my most imperfect writing. Without him by my side, I know I wouldn't have had the courage to submit *Ambrosia* for publication, let alone re-publish it once the rights were returned to me.

I'm fortunate to have been part of several writing communities that have helped me grow in my craft. The Northwest Indiana-based group Quilling Time was my rock throughout writing, editing, and publishing this novel. From advising me through specific issues to simply serving as a sounding board, they were there for me. Specifically, I'm grateful for Rhonda Zetazalo and Casey Perry, who worked as beta readers for me; I admire them as writers and as people; during my time in Indiana, they inspired me to write with honesty and courage, and I'm so glad to know them.

Before querying *Ambrosia*, I had help from members of the online writing community. I'm grateful to members of Scribophile who critiqued early versions of *Ambrosia*, specifically Delia Talent, Tate Marie, Elle Turpitt, T.K. Forrester, Jennifer Grace, and M.L. Yates. I'm also grateful for my developmental editor Melissa Kaye, whose detailed, constructive feedback helped me to expand the original novelette into the novel you've just read.

I'm immensely grateful to the Authors 4 Authors Publishing team, who published the first edition of *Ambrosia*. From the moment I received word that they wanted to publish *Ambrosia*, I knew that this novel would be in good hands. It was an honor working with Rebecca Mikkelson, Brandi Spencer, and Renee Frey, fantastic human beings with a heart for stories and the authors who tell them. I appreciate the hard work they put into helping me to polish this story and share it with the world. Additionally, I want to thank Karen Heenan, who was always available to answer my questions about transitioning from from traditional publishing to self-publishing; she also introduced me to Dee Dee Book Covers, who crafted a vibrant and stunning new cover to commemorate *Ambrosia's* new release.

Lastly, I want to thank you, the reader. I've poured my heart into this project, and I appreciate that you took the time to read and review it.

Most importantly, I'm grateful that God put me on this writing journey in the first place. It has been a joy thus far, and I can't wait to see where it leads.

Interlude: Through a Glass, Darkly

Don't look, don't look, don't look...

But the smell of Luca's blood calls to me, luring my eyes toward the scene I've tried so hard to avoid. Metallic, harsh—there's so much blood.

My right hand clenches around the glass shard I'd used to kill him. My left hand rakes through my frayed braids, pulling a handful up by the roots as I try not to cry.

I have to look. Not just to appease my guilty conscience, but to see if it *worked.*

Was my sacrifice all in vain?

My grip around the shard tightens, drawing my own blood, which intermingles with Luca's.

Look, dammit! My eyes snap open, and my focus shifts reluctantly to the body. I back away instinctively, my stomach churning. Leaning against the bedroom wall, I cover my mouth with one hand to suppress the sob that forms in my throat. Blood, like war paint, covers the lower half of my face.

My head spins, making me collapse onto my bed. Curling my knees to my chest, I force myself to keep looking, though every cell in my body demands that I run far, far away.

As if something as inconsequential as distance could erase what I have done.

So I look. I make myself observe the expression of glassy-eyed betrayal permanently etched into my boyfriend's face. The way the color slowly drains from his once-bronze skin. The wounds bleed out, pooling around him and staining the white carpet.

And towering over Luca's body like some cold, hungry idol is the Mirror. I'm afraid to look into its reflective surface, knowing it will only magnify this awful reality.

"*Look.*" The Mirror's voice echoes in my mind, soft yet unyielding. Whimpering, I glance up. The woman in the mirror appears small. Fragile. This isn't what I had been promised. There's no sudden surge of power coursing through my veins, no transformation. Just a bitter hollowness in my chest as I come to terms with my reality.

I murdered Luca...and it was all for nothing.

I rise and approach the Mirror. The familiar crackle of energy radiates from its surface, making the hair on my arms rise up. I watch, my eyes shining with tears as I wait for something—anything—to happen.

Because I hadn't been imagining things.

Because I'm not going crazy.

Because I *will* get what I've been promised.

I take another step toward the Mirror, my hands balling into defiant fists. "You promised!" I punctuate the accusation with a useless punch to the glass.

But still, my reflection doesn't change.

I rain blow after angry blow to the glass, my voice ragged and raw as I scream, sinking to the bloody floor.

Only now...the blood is gone.

I scramble away from the Mirror, startled by the sudden absence of blood. The absence of Luca.

He's vanished, along with any other evidence of my crime.

Looking up, I see my reflection looming over me, her perfectly manicured nail beckoning toward me. I stand, trembling, taking hesitant steps toward the Mirror.

The glass reflects the dim light of my room, but the woman behind it is *not me.* Those eyes lack the fear that widens mine like little moons. Her straight, dark hair tumbles gracefully past her waist. A secretive smile slowly crawls up her face as I continue my terrified walk toward the Mirror. Once I'm only a few feet away, the woman points downward.

And it's behind the glass that I see Luca, his blood surrounding his motionless body like a dark halo.

"Well done," the woman purrs, her left hand reflecting mine as it grips the bloody shard that I had wielded moments before.

The world momentarily tilts as I'm overcome by a wave of nausea. I can't seem to look away from the body behind the glass. Tears flow again as I sink to the floor again, my head pressed against the cold glass as I whisper, "I'm so sorry, Luc…"

The figure stoops down to my level, holding up a bloody hand as if in silent invitation. "He held us back, Nailah. You know this."

I shake my head, staring past this uncanny version of myself. "No. You tricked me."

My alternate tilts her head, as if I'd said something truly confounding. "Tricked you? This was *your* choice. And you know why you did it."

I focus on Luca's still figure, trying to block out my alternate's words.

"Nailah," she whispers. "Look at me."

I sniffle, tentatively looking up to meet the reflection's intense gaze. For half a second, her eyes change color, the warm brown replaced by a harsh silver.

My alternate says in a cold, flat tone, "What's done is done. The sacrifice is complete. You can't bring him back."

I nod, the statement making my heart sink.

"But you can make sure that his death wasn't in vain," she continues. "You can do what you set out to do, become who you deserve to be."

She offers her hand to me, leaving a bloody handprint on the glass as she waits for me to take it. Blinking back a fresh wave of tears, I reach out to touch her hand but hesitate. I glance back at Luca, the ache in my chest intensifying as I'm haunted by memories of the life we'd had.

My alternate sighs and rubs her temples, leaving bloody fingerprints on her otherwise perfect skin. I try to turn away, but her voice snaps like a whip. "I said, *look at me.*"

My head jerks up against my will. The woman's expression hardens, her eyes piercing—briefly flashing with silver once again.

"I've promised you that the path I've set you down will result in great rewards," she says, her voice low and conspiratorial. "And I always keep my promises. Do you believe this?"

"Yes," I whisper, not daring to look away from the reflection.

"Good. But remember, it's a *path.* A journey. And he..." She gestures to Luca's corpse. "He's just the first of many sacrifices."

Bile rises to my throat as the weight of her statement settles in. "No. No, that's not what you told me."

She shrugs, her expression unapologetic. "You want to walk away, don't you? You want to abandon this path."

"Y-yes," I whisper weakly, taking a few backward steps as in emphasis. "This isn't what I...signed up for."

She removes her hand from the glass, her backward steps mirroring mine as she prepares to withdraw. But then, a thoughtful look crosses her face. "Very well. I'll leave. But first...a little reminder."

My mouth falls open in protest. But before the words come out, the Mirror reveals another version of me: my childhood self. Her hair is frizzy and wild, full of tangles and locks that speak of neglect. The child's wide eyes shine with tears as she stares up at me with a questioning look. And I know the questions that linger behind those eyes all too well.

"Why doesn't Mommy love me?"

"When is Daddy coming home?"

"Why don't I matter?"

I reach out as if to touch the reflected image, but what could I possibly do to comfort this version of myself? Tell her that everything will be okay? That she'll emerge from this dysfunctional childhood unscathed?

Should I lie?

My hand shakes as I reach for the reflection. But a sudden cacophony from beyond the glass makes me withdraw. Raised voices intermingling. Siblings screaming and laughing and crying for attention. My mother's harsh, shrill voice rising above the noise. Doors slamming. Glass shattering. And amidst all this chaos, this vision of my childhood self remains silent. Silenced by fear and uncertainty, unsure of how to attract the attention she so desperately needs.

A tear slips down my cheek. I don't bother wiping it away.

The vision vanishes, replaced by the reflection of my alternate, her perfect face downcast, her sculpted brows knit together in contempt. "We never really figured out how to stand out, did we?"

"No. We just kind of...got lost in the shuffle."

"Lost in the shuffle," my reflection repeats. "No wonder we're attention whores."

I scoff, wincing at the phrase that had been wielded at me all too often throughout high school. "Attention whore. Dramatic. Shallow."

"No one understood why," my alternate muses. She jerks her head toward Luca. "Not even him."

"How could he?" I say, my gaze flicking toward him for a moment. "He had a *perfect childhood.*"

She nods, her brow furrowing in resentment. "He never had to beg for affection. For attention."

"For love." But even as I wrestle with that all too familiar envy of Luca's life, I stiffen, reminding myself that he didn't deserve to die.

That it's not his fault that I'm damaged.

As if reading my thoughts, the woman in the Mirror gives me a gentle smile and says, "One last thing before I go. I know you're hesitant, but I would be remiss if I didn't show you what you could be missing out on."

The reflection changes again, showing me flashes of a brighter future, like a montage from a movie scene. There's my social media account, revealing an army of followers. There's me, speaking in front of a crowd of adoring fans. There I am, taking a selfie as I lounge on my yacht. There I am, laughing with a group of friends as we knock back fruity drinks in a bar. Scene after scene plays before me, and in each of them, the smile never leaves my face. Not ever.

I draw closer to the Mirror, reaching out as if to step through the glass and into the charmed life that these images promise.

But my fingertips brush against the glass, a cold, tangible reminder that these are just visions. Illusions of what could be.

Unless...

The montage ends, leaving me breathless with envy.

"It's not too late." My alternate looks at me with sisterly affection. "You've already taken the most difficult step." She lifts her hand for a third time, pressing it against the glass in one final invitation. "You don't have to be afraid."

I grip the shard tighter, its bite a stark reminder of what I've done—and what I'll do next.

My alternate stares, awaiting my decision. Her voice cracks a bit as she says, "You don't have to be alone anymore."

I grit my teeth, the words cutting deep.

Because she's right—I am an attention whore. But it's never been about a shallow need for recognition. It's never been about my own fucking ego.

It's always been about feeling alone.

I drop the glass fragment. As it thuds softly against the carpet, my bloodstained hand drifts upward to meet hers. And when it does, I feel her flesh—sticky with Luca's blood—instead of glass. Before I can react, her hand closes on mine.

"Hold on," she commands. "And keep still."

So I tighten my grip around hers as the transformation takes hold, subtly at first. Warmth spreads from our joined hands, an electric heat curling through my veins. It prickles my skin, sharp and invigorating, as if lightning had struck me and left me glowing. Brightening my skin as if with some mysterious inner light. Smoothing every blemish, every scar. A sensation like electricity makes me stand up straighter—adding inches to my height. My stomach flattens, and when I put my hand to my abdomen, I can feel unearned muscles, as if I've spent months toiling away at the gym.

My skin prickles with goosebumps as I watch the transformation take hold. I lift my hand to my scalp, feeling the frizzy braids melt away, replaced by impossibly silky locks. Moving my hand to my roots, tugging them to test whether they're real.

My alternate's smile matches mine as I marvel at the metamorphosis. Once again, my eyes flash with a steely light for a brief moment before resuming their normal shade.

"The change isn't just physical, though, is it?" she asks.

"No...I feel different."

"More confident," she says.

"More confident. Like I could easily conquer the world."

My alternate gives me that secretive smile she'd given before. But now...I understand the mystery it had held. "Well, then," she says. "Let's conquer the world."

Still basking in the glow of my transformation, I ask, "What do I do?"

"You'll see."

Nailah's transformation is just beginning. Her story continues in the sequel to Ambrosia, coming soon!

About the Author

Madison Wheatley is a poet, fiction writer, and author of the debut paranormal thriller novel *Ambrosia*. She specializes in speculative fiction where the paranormal and psychological collide. Her short fiction has been featured in *Seven Deadly Sins, A YA Anthology: Avarice* and *Secrets in Our Cities: A Paranormal Urban Fantasy Anthology*. When she's not writing, Madison works as a high school English teacher and yearbook adviser, nurturing the next generation of storytellers. She lives in Southern Delaware with her husband, cat, and two dogs.

You can connect with me on:

- http://www.madisonwheatley.com
- https://www.facebook.com/mwheatleywriter
- https://www.instagram.com/mwheatleywriter
- https://www.threads.net/@mwheatleywriter

Subscribe to my newsletter:

- https://madisonwheatley.beehiiv.com/subscribe